FIRE IN THE SNOW

Slocum was just about to hold a lucifer to the end of his smoke when he saw movement in the trees. Riders!

He whistled a birdcall, hoping that at least one of the Harper boys would hear him, and luckily, one did. Slocum had to hand it to them. They all went in real casual, just like it was about suppertime and they were all going in to eat. Just like he'd told them to.

At last, the first rider came into full view. Then Mitcham, then that son-of-a-bitch, Blackfoot.

They were circling the little house like a pack of wolves, and suddenly, Slocum realized why. He saw first one fiery torch, then another, sail up from behind the house to land on its roof. Mitcham tossed a third flaming torch through the side window. Below, out front of the house, Siler raised his rifle and waited.

Slocum did the only thing he could do in these circumstances. He fired once and Siler dropped before getting off a shot.

He wasn't dead, though, and when the Harper boys and their dog came out of the house, the dog went right to Siler and pinned him before he could reach for his gun. All three of the other men were armed, and they fired wildly, their smoke-teared eyes unable to see where they were aiming.

JAKE LOGAN

SLOCUM
THE GUNMAN AND
THE GREENHORN

J
JOVE BOOKS, NEW YORK

This is a work of fiction. Names, characters, places, and incidents either are the product of the author's imagination or are used fictitiously, and any resemblance to actual persons, living or dead, business establishments, events, or locales is entirely coincidental.

THE GUNMAN AND THE GREENHORN

A Jove Book / published by arrangement with the author

PRINTING HISTORY
Jove edition / December 2003

ISBN: 0-515-13639-5

A JOVE BOOK®
Jove Books are published by The Berkley Publishing Group, a division of Penguin Group (USA) Inc., 375 Hudson Street, New York, New York 10014.
JOVE and the "J" design are trademarks belonging to Penguin Group (USA) Inc.

PRINTED IN THE UNITED STATES OF AMERICA

10 9 8 7 6 5 4 3 2 1

1

Mad as hell and riding at a dead gallop, Slocum skittered his gelding sideways down the side of a steep arroyo, then leapt from the horse's back.

He yanked his Winchester from its boot, then smacked the Appaloosa across his speckled rump, sending him on to where the arroyo was deeper and he'd be hidden. And only then did he turn his attention—and his guns—to the goddamn fool who was shooting at him.

No, he corrected himself: the fool who had shot him already.

On his belly, his arm stinging, he pulled himself up toward the top of the arroyo's side. He tossed down his sweat-stained hat at the last minute and drew his pistol, then peeked out. The goddamn lunatic was sitting right there, just out of gun range.

But not rifle range.

He seemed to be listening to the slowing sound of Tubac's hoofbeats, because just then he urged his mount on—and away—to parallel the dry creek bed.

He didn't get far, though.

Slocum brought up his rifle, allowed for the wind and the distance for his slug to land right in the middle of the man's hat, and squeezed the trigger.

1

He hadn't lost his touch, he thought with a satisfied grunt as he saw the man's tan Stetson suddenly fly into the air and dance on the breeze. At the same moment, the fellow who'd been stalking him yelped and grabbed the top of his head.

Well, maybe a touch off, Slocum thought with a shrug, then smiled smugly as he thought about the new—and permanent—part he'd put in the son of a bitch's hair.

The man wheeled his horse back toward Slocum, but before he could bring that rifle of his up, another well-placed shot from Slocum knocked the long gun from his hands, singing quite audibly off the barrel. The man's right hand automatically went to his mouth, but he still managed to scramble off his horse. He started to run for cover.

A third shot from Slocum's Winchester hit the dirt two feet ahead in the fellow's path. That one stopped him cold.

"You ain't an easy one to convince," Slocum shouted. "Just hold the hell still!"

"Go ahead and shoot me, Mitcham!" the young man shouted back. He turned and flung his arms wide, presenting his chest. "You already got my brothers, go ahead and shoot the whole damned family!"

Slocum's brow furrowed. "Who's this Mitcham you're blatherin' about?"

"Quit playin' cat and mouse, you son of a skunk," the man called back. Slocum could tell now that he was in his mid twenties, blond, and fairly tall, almost as tall as Slocum was. "I been followin' your tracks for three days now!"

"Well, you been followin' the wrong set, kid," Slocum called. "My name's Slocum, and I ain't shot nobody on purpose for at least a month and a half. Now, you want to calm down and parley, or you want to stand out there in the sun all day?"

"I ain't no kid!" came the reply.

"Fine," shouted Slocum. "Stand there, then."

Exactly two very long minutes went by before the boy called, "You sure you ain't Jack Mitcham?"

"Not unless my daddy was lyin' to me," Slocum said.

"All right," said the boy, lowering his arms. "Parley."

"Fine. Just drop those handguns of yours in the dirt first. If'n you don't mind. And then back off a few steps."

The boy shrugged, then grudgingly complied and took a couple of steps backward. "Happy?"

Slocum scrambled the rest of the way over the crest of the arroyo's wall. "Fair to middlin'." He stood up. "You winged me back there, you know."

The boy seemed genuinely surprised to see the blood staining the blue of Slocum's shirtsleeve. He blinked, and said, "You didn't give no sign."

In lieu of an answer, Slocum said, "Go and fetch your damn hat and your horse."

While the kid walked to get his Stetson, Slocum whistled up Tubac, then picked up the kid's guns and stuck them in his belt. He picked up the boy's rifle, too. It was no good anymore, unless the kid wanted to blow himself to Kingdom Come. Slocum's slug had put a sizable dent in the barrel. Any bullet fired through it would simply stop at the dent, ricochet back and forth and, in the process, shatter it.

And probably the shooter, too.

Tubac came up over the side of the arroyo some distance away and started picking his way toward Slocum at about the same time that the kid started back with his hat. He had one forefinger stuck through each of the exit and entry holes, and was shaking his head. Slocum noticed that his noggin was bleeding profusely, too. Scalp wounds always did.

"You got a name?" Slocum asked as the kid neared.

"Josh," the kid said. "Joshua Quaid." He looked up from his hat. "You coulda killed me, mister!" he announced, having gotten over the shock of it enough to be angry.

"Didn't though, did I?" Slocum said, then added, "C'mere, let me take a look at that head of yours."

Josh's eyes narrowed with suspicion. "Why should I?"

" 'Cause, in case you haven't noticed, you're gonna bleed all over yourself if you don't."

Josh put a hand to his head, and it came away dripping red. He wobbled a little, as if he were going to pass out.

And he did. He just crumpled up right there, and went down on his ass on the desert floor.

Slocum shook his head. "What're we gettin' ourselves into, Tubac?" he asked the horse, which was just ambling up to him. Slocum slid his rifle back into its boot while the bay leopard Appy nuzzled his back pocket, looking for sugar.

"Wrong pocket," Slocum said absently, and pulled a sugar lump from his vest pocket. He gave it to the horse, who munched contentedly, and then he turned his attention to his saddlebags.

He pulled out a clean cloth, took the finest needle he could find from his sewing kit—which was most often used for mending busted tack—pulled a longish hair from Tubac's tail and grabbed his canteen.

"Just as well you passed out, Josh, my boy," he muttered as he slowly walked over to the body. He squinted, concentrating on threading the horse hair through the eye of the needle. "This is gonna smart a mite."

As it happened, Josh came directly out of his swoon about fifteen seconds after Slocum started to wash the site of the wound, but a good pop on the jaw knocked him out again.

Slocum wasn't much for stitching up thrashing patients. It was hard enough work when they lay still.

The job completed to his satisfaction and the last of the long horse hair bitten off, he surveyed his work. Young Mr. Joshua Quaid might have himself a crookedy part for the rest of his life, but at least he wouldn't have a crooked part consisting of a couple inches of scar tissue with his skull practically showing through.

With nothing else to do, Slocum went through the kid's pockets. He was out of Iowa—at least, that's what the battered picture in the wallet said on the back. In it, he was standing up all straight and un-smiling alongside two other fellows. All three were slicked and spit-shined for the occasion.

Josh Quaid sure wasn't rich, either. He had two dollars and change in his purse, and a gold eagle sewn into the lining of his jacket. That last part spoke vol-umes to Slocum, who only sewed large sums into his clothes. For instance, on those occasions when he was carrying a thousand dollars or more.

Night was going to come on within the next couple of hours and Josh was still as out as a cold oil lamp, so Slocum stripped both their horses of tack and wa-tered, brushed and groomed, then fed them. The kid's horse was a nice bay: not flashy, though. Only a white snip on his nose and a left rear coronet. He seemed well-put-together enough.

After he secured the horses and put the nose bags away, Slocum gathered kindling and wood for a fire. Out here, there was plenty of dead brush to choose from, although a man had to watch out for rattle-snakes sheltering in the shade.

To the west, the sky was just beginning to take on tinges of orange and red and salmon pink when he at last built the fire and lit it, and placed the coffeepot to heat on a flat rock at the edge of the blaze. He was just pulling out fixings for supper—the makings for biscuits, plus a few vegetables for stew and a rabbit he'd shot just before Josh Quaid started shooting at him—when the kid came to.

One hand went to his head even before he opened his eyes, and he scowled as if in great pain.

"Feel tight?" Slocum asked. He was skinning the jackrabbit.

"Heck, yes," mutter Josh. "What'd you do to me, anyhow? I kinda remember . . . Did you slug me?"

"Guilty," said Slocum, intent on the rabbit. "You were wakin' up. Trust me, you didn't want to be doin' that just then."

The kid's hand went to his jaw, which was swelling and purpled. "I'm gonna be bruised."

Slocum shrugged. "You are already. But I did a mighty fine job of stitchin' up your noggin, if I do say so myself."

"Can't tell," came the irritated reply. "You tied a damned bandage on it."

Slocum ignored the kid's bitching and began cutting the rabbit into pieces. He wasn't the best campfire cook, not by a longshot, but he knew how to make a few things pretty well. Rabbit stew was one of them, and one of his favorites, too.

When he'd passed through Paso Robles a couple of days before, he'd stocked up on incidentals, like carrots and potatoes and onions and such, but all he'd shot to go with them was a quail. He was really looking forward to this meal.

He poured water into a pan and set it on the fire, then added the chunks of rabbit and vegetables, a little salt and a lot of pepper, then stuck a lid on it. His stomach was beginning to growl.

Well, it'd just have to growl about an hour longer, that was all. He grabbed the last carrot and began to chew on it, raw, to tide him over.

Jaws crunching, he lounged back against the saddle at the head of his bedroll.

"So," he said. "Tell me your story, Josh. We got about an hour to kill before that stew's done, and I've gotta admit, I'm right curious. How'd you come to mistake my trail for this Mitcham feller's, anyhow?"

2

"I been thinkin' about that," Josh said softly, staring into the cook fire. "I ain't been out all this time, you know. Been cogitatin' on it."

He pushed his bullet-riddled hat back on his head, but gently, so as not to disturb the bandages on his scalp.

"And you come up with . . . ?" Slocum urged.

"Guess it musta been back in Paso Robles," Josh replied, more to himself than to Slocum. "Don't know how I coulda done it, but it sure looks like I did. Mister, you don't look nothin' like Jack Mitcham, once a feller gets up close."

"Just call me Slocum, Josh," Slocum said.

"You still don't look much like him," the kid went on blithely. "I'd sure like to get my hands on that son of a bitch, though. I suppose now I've gotta start all over." His face twisted. "Aw, green apples and horse shit!"

A small stick, which he'd just picked up from the ground, went sailing past Slocum's right ear, and Slocum gruffly said, "Watch it."

"Sorry," Josh said with a shrug. "Didn't look where I was throwin'."

"You said he killed your brothers," Slocum coaxed,

9

hoping to get him back on the subject at hand.

Josh's face suddenly dropped, and there was a long moment of silence before he said, "Earl and Joe. Earl was older than me and Joe was a couple years younger. Us three was out on the trail."

Slocum figured those must be the other two in the picture. He waited, and while he waited, he dug for his tobacco pouch and fixings.

Finally, Josh went on. "We come from Iowa, seekin' our fortune. Or somethin.' Pa said it was a young feller's right to go off and sow a few wild oats," he added defensively.

Slocum, rolling a quirlie, nodded. "That it is."

Absently, Slocum wondered just when the cutoff for "young" was. He was, after all, past forty now, and he still hadn't gotten over the urge to keep moving, see what was over the next horizon.

And the next.

And the next.

"Well, we was in Colorado Springs when we got the wire," Josh went on. "Ma died. Fever. First Ma, then Pa went a couple days later."

As a pair of coyotes gave voice in the distance, Slocum lit his quirlie. "You make it sound like you coulda done somethin' if you was there. Somethin' besides dyin' yourself, that is."

The boy stared at his knees.

Funny, Slocum thought, how he kept thinking of Josh as "the boy" or "the kid." When Slocum had been twenty-five or so, he'd been through a terrible war and seen—and done—more hell than most men do in a lifetime, if they're lucky. If anybody had been so foolish as to call him a kid, the party in question would have suffered immediate consequences.

And they wouldn't have been pretty.

Still, he couldn't help himself. He asked, "So what happened to your brothers? After you heard about your folks."

Josh sighed. "Well, we didn't go back home. That was, to Iowa. Folks had already been buried and the words spoke over them a long time before we got word. So we just kept ridin', and we rode our way down to Flagstaff. Thought we might get some ranch work up, or mayhap somethin' to do on the railroad."

He stopped again, and Slocum figured that they were closer to it, but still no cigar.

"And?" he asked, taking a draw on his smoke.

"We was in the Bird's Eye Saloon," Josh finally went on. "It's just a little hole-in-the-wall place. Five, maybe six tables, and narrow as a shoe box."

"I know the place," Slocum said.

The Bird's Eye was indeed narrow, although he would have described it more like a narrow-gauge freight car than a shoe box. Just enough room for the bar to run down one side, and the little tables to be pressed up against the opposite wall.

"We was in there, at the bar, when this feller came up to us and took exception to something that Earl said. Can't even remember what it was. Don't you think I'd remember somethin' like that, Slocum? But for the life of me . . ."

Once again, the boy drifted off into silence. Slocum took advantage of the situation to lift the lid and give the stew a stir. It was smelling mighty good. He poured himself a steaming cup of Arbuckle's, then thought twice and offered it to the kid.

Who took it.

He poured out another for himself, took a careful sip, then said, "I'm takin' it that this feller was Jack Mitcham?"

"Yeah," Josh said bitterly. Both hands were clasped around his enameled coffee cup, and he didn't look up from it.

"He said something," the kid went on, "then Earl said somethin' and Joe backed him up on it. We was standing all in a line, Earl and Joe and me, with me bein' at the rear. Mitcham got mad and said something bad about our mama and our papa and our ancestry in general, and that's when Earl slugged him. Tried to, anyhow."

Josh sucked on his upper lip for a second. "Never seen nothin' like it and I never hope to again. That son of a bitch, Mitcham, ducked under Earl's punch so that he hit nothin' but air, and at the same time, Mitcham drew his gun. I remember he had him a pair of eagle-butt Colts, one on each hip. I remember thinking they was real handsome when he first come in and ordered his whiskey and beer chaser."

Josh paused to take a sip of his coffee. "Anyhow,

he fired. Gut-shot both Earl and Joe, and I stopped the bullet with my rib cage. Lucky, I guess. I remember Mitcham laughin' and sayin' as how he believed in savin' ammunition, and it looked like he'd done right by himself with that handgun slug. 'Three for the price of one!' he said, fairly crowing. Course, it was right about then that I passed out."

Josh flushed straight up his neck and into his cheeks. "I never been much good at the sight of blood, I guess. Especially my own. It got so that back home, Pa always sent me to the opposite end of the farm when it came hog or steer butcherin' time. Hell, I'd even pass out if I saw Ma chop off a chicken's head."

"No shame in that," Slocum lied. "Some folks ain't built to take it."

Josh seemed to know it was a fib, because he said, "Thanks for tryin' to make me feel better. But I don't. Anyhow, when I come to at the doc's they told me that Earl had already gone to heaven and Joe didn't have long. He lasted just until I got in there and took hold of his hand."

He paused and gulped, his Adam's apple bobbing. "Poor Joe looked up at me, him all pumped fulla opium painkillers and still sufferin' terrible, and said, 'Get that bastard for this, Josh. Get him for Earl an' me.' And then he died, just like that."

Slocum let the kid eat half his meal before he started talking again. Josh was half-starved by the looks of it, and was into his second plate when Slocum said, "I think that maybe I know this Jack Mitcham of yours."

Josh stopped, mid-chew.

"Big fella, dark hair? About thirty-five, forty?"

Josh swallowed with some difficulty and said, "Yup."

"Got a long, crooked scar, runs from above his eyebrow and halfway down his cheek, just misses his eyeball?"

"That's him! Why the hell didn't you say somethin', Slocum?"

Slocum shrugged. "Didn't dawn on me till you said as how he was big on savin' ammunition. One time, I watched him rope four Mexicans up in a row and take 'em out with one rifle shot, the sleazy son of a bitch. I wasn't in any position to do anything about it then," he added.

As a matter of fact, Slocum had been pinned down by gunfire and out of ammo himself when Mitcham and his boys came to call on the town of Jaguar Springs that day. Without thinking, he rubbed a hand over the scar on his side, the long one left by Mitcham's bullet.

He sighed deeply, then looked up. "But I believe I am now."

Josh's jaw dropped practically to his chest, and then he snapped it shut with a *click*. "You . . . you're goin' with me?" he asked, as if he couldn't believe his good fortune.

"No," Slocum replied, picking up another forkful of stew, this one with a bug chunk of potato in it. "You're goin' with me."

"But—"

"Don't 'but' me, Josh. You already managed to lose him once." Slocum took a bite and chewed it thoughtfully while Josh waited, leaning forward anxiously.

Slocum finally swallowed. It was mighty good stew.

"I been lookin' for this piece a shit for over ten years, off and on," he said. "Almost ran across him once or twice, but always lost him. This time," he said, pausing to take another drink of coffee, "he ain't gonna get lost. Not again."

"Well, how the hell you reckon to find him?" Josh replied indignantly. "Like I told you, I lost him back in Paso Robles. Followed your tracks out here, because I thought he was you. Same weight, same shoe prints on his horse. 'Bout the same size boot, too, when he got down to tend his horse."

Slocum nodded. The kid was a fairly good tracker, then. He'd give him that. And he'd likely come in handy. He had as much—if not more—of a grudge against Mitcham than Slocum did.

Sort of.

"I'll tell you something about this Mitcham of yours, Josh," Slocum said.

Above, a night-hunting bird screeched as it dived

swiftly toward its helpless prey. Neither man gave it so much as a glance.

"Back when I knew him," Slocum continued, "he was callin' himself Rod Miles. He was a mercenary, for sale to anybody who wanted him. I don't mean a bounty hunter or a hired gun. I mean, a real live mercenary. Hired himself out for range wars or personal vendettas, didn't matter if the side that hired him was in the wrong or in the right."

Slocum paused, his face growing dark. "To say that he enjoys killin' is puttin' it mild. Probably got a real kick out of murderin' your brothers. And if he runs across you, alone in the desert, he's liable to plug you, too, just to finish the job. Keep his record perfect, so to speak."

For once, Josh was speechless.

"So you're goin' along with me," Slocum continued. "And the first place we're goin' is back to Paso Robles. That's where you lost him, and that's where we'll go to pick up his trail."

"How you gonna do that?" Josh fairly yelped. "The trail's old now! It's probably disappeared by now!"

Slocum poured himself another cup of coffee. "Got ways," he said, then took a sip. "Hope you're not one'a those full-of-religion types."

Josh's face twisted. "Why?"

" 'Cause we're gonna spend at least a night at the whorehouse, that's why."

"A whorehouse?" Josh replied, his features twisting. Slocum couldn't tell if he was just scared, never having seen the inside of one before, or if he was going to make the sign of the cross.

"You'd be surprised what you can find out from those ladies of the night," Slocum said. "And I happen to be on pretty good terms with the madam up at the Paso Robles Pleasure Palace. You gettin' the picture, kid?"

"Yeah, I guess so," replied Josh. "And do me a favor, Slocum? Don't call me kid."

3

As the men traveled for the next couple of days, they got to know each other better. Or at least, Slocum learned more about Josh Quaid.

He'd come from a little bit of a town just outside Des Moines, Iowa, where his family had a farm in the Raccoon Valley, alongside the Raccoon River. Slocum gathered it was pretty good land, because there was always a hint—or more—of a brag in Josh's voice every time he spoke about their perpetually high corn yields, or how well the hogs did, or how fat the cattle grew.

"Why, it's so emerald green there in the spring and summer, the color just about blinds a man," Josh said. "And not just emerald. Every shade of green that a man can think of, and all piled on top of each other. There's lots of trees along the river. My daddy built our house without havin' to go more'n sixty yards to fell the last log!"

It had been a long time since Slocum had been in any part of the countryside answering that description, so green and verdant. A little part of him was kind of jealous.

Josh had an aunt and uncle who were still alive, so far as he knew, letters taking quite a while to travel out west, especially when you couldn't really nail down a traveling man's address. But Josh had written them when his brothers were killed and he was wounded.

"Hardest thing I ever writ in my life," he said sadly. "Poor Aunt Sarah and Uncle Amos. Ma and Pa goin' like they did, and now Earl and Joe gettin' murdered. Aunt Sarah and Uncle Amos ain't got no kids of their own. They . . . they just had us."

"You stick around long enough to get a reply?" Slocum asked.

Josh just shook his head. "I wanted to get on that killer's trail soon as I could. The next time I write home, I want it to be to say that I killed that murderin' skunk. And that I'm comin' home to take over Pa's farm. Uncle Amos is trying to see to both of 'em right now. It's a big job, and he's gettin' on."

At first, Slocum was a tad surprised that Josh was wanting to go back home. But then, Slocum had perpetually itchy feet. Josh might just be the sort whose toes tickled him only in his youth. Plus, seeing both his brothers gunned down might have scratched that itch for good.

Slocum had a feeling that was the case.

He also found out that Josh was good with horses, which sat just fine with Slocum. He asked all kinds of questions about Tubac, never having seen a Paloos horse before, and in between answering him, Slocum found out that his little bay gelding's name was Stoney, and that he was six years old. Josh had raised

him from a colt, back on that Iowa farm, and he was
from Morgan stock.

"Bet he's surefooted as all get out," Slocum commented.

"Yup," Josh answered. "He's a good'un. Reins
with the best of 'em and turns on a bottle stopper."
Proudly, he patted the bay on his neck.

"Pretty headed, too," Slocum said, admiringly. The
bay had little ears, tipped inward, and wide-set, big,
brown, intelligent eyes. Probably had a good dose of
Arabian in him.

"That he is," came the answer.

Josh also played the harmonica, and entertained
Slocum on a couple of occasions with old-time songs
like "Lorena" or "O Daddy Dear, the Crops Are
Failin' " or "Six Goats on a Mountain" or "Old Black
Joe." He played them just fine, with plenty of feeling
and just the right flourishes here and there.

And when he played "My Alabama Home," it
nearly brought Slocum to tears.

At least, he felt a little heat pushing behind his
eyes.

They rode into Paso Robles at about four-thirty the
second afternoon, and Slocum was pleased to see that
Josh rode straight to the livery to settle in his horse,
instead of to the saloon to settle the dust in his own
throat. The saloon would have been most men's first
port of call.

After they settled the horses in, Slocum had a chat
with his old friend Jim Cassidy, who ran the livery,

and then they hiked up the street to the Roadrunner Café, where they ordered a good supper. Slocum had himself a medium rare steak with all the fixings, and Josh had the fried chicken dinner.

He said it was real crispy and good. Must have been, too, by the way he mopped up that plate. He even cleaned the gristle off the ends of the bones, and then had seconds on dessert.

At last, it came time to pay a call up at the Paso Robles Pleasure Palace, and that was the first time in two days that Slocum saw Josh put the brakes on just a little.

"Sure we shouldn't stop back and check on the horses first?" he said.

"They're fine. Jim Cassidy'll take good care of 'em. You can count on that."

"Well, shouldn't we stop and get a shave first?" Josh asked.

"Barbershop's closed," Slocum said, trying not to grin. " 'Sides, you can get a shave up at Miss Mandy's place."

"Mandy?"

"At the Paso Robles Pleasure Palace."

"Well, shouldn't we even take a bath or some-thin'?" The kid just wouldn't give up. "I swan, Slo-cum, we smell like a paira billy goats!"

Slocum stopped walking, and Josh stopped with him.

"All right," he said as patiently as he could. "Josh, I've taken a liking to you for some crazy reason, which is why I'm not gonna punch you through a wall for makin' that billy goat crack. Hell, you ever smelled one up close? They smell like six years of piss."

If there had been dirt on the boardwalk to dig his toe into, Josh would have. As it was, he just looked at his feet and said, "Naw, we didn't have no goats. Sorry."

"All right. I know we're both kinda rank, but don't exaggerate so wild. They got bathtubs up at Mindy's place, too. And bein' as I figure it to be Thursday night, there ain't gonna be much of a rush on 'em. Same goes for the gals."

Josh gulped. "But I ain't never—"

"You mean to tell me," Slocum interrupted, "that you ain't never been with a woman?" His brows were hoisted so high that he felt them lifting his damned hat!

"Sure!" Josh replied angrily. "Sure I been! Lotsa times. Plenty! I just never been with one when I was so hog-dirty, that's all!" And then he paused. He looked at the ground again. "Besides, I ain't got enough cash money on me. Buryin' Earl and Joe wasn't cheap, even after I sold their horses."

Slocum broke out in a big, relieved grin. Thank God he hadn't been riding for two days with a virgin. Nothin' wrong with it, of course, but he thought he should've known or something.

His faith in his judgment of human nature reaffirmed, he said, "Hell, Josh, I'm pretty flush. Consider it my present for helpin' to ferret out that murderin' skunk, Rod Miles. Or Jack Mitcham. Or whatever he's callin' himself now. So live it up, son. Have yourself a bath. Have yourself a shave. Have two women. Have three!"

"No shit?" Josh said, a smile beginning to tickle at one corner of his mouth.

"No shit," replied Slocum with a laugh. He slapped Josh on the back, and the two of them proceeded up the street to the Paso Robles Pleasure Palace.

And, of course, the lovely Mandy Summers.

When they walked into the Paso Robles Pleasure Palace, Josh was greeted by the sound of somebody playing a piano in another room, the sight of a whole lot of gals in their underwear sitting around on pink or red velvet sofas and the smell of a yellow haze of cigar smoke. Most of which was coming from the gals.

Now, Josh was a little shocked. He and his brothers had taken themselves to a house of ill repute the second they crossed the state line into Nebraska, but it sure had been different than this. It was all fancy mahogany woodwork and ladies who looked more like, well, ladies.

He had lost his virginity there to a pretty little gal named Roxanne, and she'd been just as nice as she could be. He'd even written her a couple of letters after he and his brothers moved on, but she never answered.

Earl laughed at him for even picking up the pen in the first place, but Joe said he guessed those gals were just too busy to write back. Why, they must get fan letters from all over the place!

He'd been with a couple of other women since then. One was a widow woman whose potato farm they stopped at for a spell, up in Colorado. She was young and pretty enough if you didn't look at that big birthmark on the side of her face, but she kept hushing him lest his brothers overhear and get all jealous.

He found out later that she'd been with all three of them, and told each one the same thing.

The other gal he'd been with had been a young Crow squaw, who just lay beneath him, cold as a piece of ice. Of course, he later learned that she was a slave, sort of, to the man who had sold him her time. It made him mad enough that he gathered up his brothers and they all went back there and gave that feller what for. Licked him pretty damn good, they did.

Then they took the gal and turned her loose and said she never had to come back to that place anymore.

They didn't have to say it twice. Once she got through her head what they were telling her—which took a while, since she didn't talk good American— she grabbed a horse out of that ramshackle barn and headed for the high country, riding bareback with her long black hair streaming out behind her.

But not before she grabbed up a handful of to-
kens—Indian things, in a little pouch—and kissed
Josh square on the jaw.

Boy, Earl and Joe teased him about that for weeks.

"You get lost on me, Josh?" Slocum was prodding
him in the side, a big grin on his face.

"Nope," he replied. "Just thinkin'." What he was
thinking about now, mostly, was that there wasn't a
one of these girls he'd even consider taking home to
meet his mama—if she were alive, that was. But there
were sure a few he'd like to get to know a little better.

That little redheaded gal back in the corner, for
instance.

Slocum must have seen him looking over there,
because he said, "Go on and talk to her. She ain't
gonna bite unless you ask her to."

Josh grabbed his hat off his head and clasped it to
his chest as Slocum was greeted by a buxom woman
old enough to be, well, Josh's aunt, anyway—and
short enough to be his daughter. He walked through
the big front room, past cigar-smoking girls, and over
to the little redhead.

Maybe, if he asked her real nice, she'd give him a
bath and a shave herself.

He blushed right down to his toes, just thinking
about it.

"Howdy, Mandy!" Slocum said, as the busty blonde
threw herself into his arms. "Long time no see."

"Long time, my fat, round ass," she replied, laughing. "You was in here, what? 'Bout five days ago? Was we so good that you just had to turn straight around and come on back?"

"That's just about it, Mandy," Slocum said with a grin. He liked Mandy. She wasn't exactly his type, seeing as she was about as tall as a ten-year-old girl and had kind of short, stumpy legs and fat hands. But he enjoyed the hell out of her company.

Mandy, who was well aware of his likes and dislikes, said, "Who's it gonna be tonight, Slocum? My Patsy's free."

"Free?" he said, lifting a brow.

Mandy smacked his elbow, which was just about as high as she could reach without raising her arm. "You old devil. You know what I mean."

"That I do, Mandy. Now, don't go roughin' me up," he added jovially. "I got a reputation to worry about."

She laughed.

He said, "Actually, I might take Patsy up on that offer she hasn't made me, but I'd kinda like to have a private parley with you, first. Kitchen all right?"

Mandy shrugged. "Sure thing. What about that kid you come in with?"

"I'm payin' for anything and anybody he wants, Mandy," he replied. "Tell that little redhead to shoot the works."

She caught the girl's eye, gestured in some sort of

signal, and suddenly the girl seemed to warm right up to Josh.

"Done," said Mandy. "Now, come on back for a cup of coffee and a gab. I think we got some cake left over from dinner, too, if'n you're interested."

4

Mandy sat back and sipped thoughtfully at her second cup of coffee. "I'll tell you the truth, Slocum," she said. "This Mitcham feller you're lookin' for? He was in here, all right, same night as you were."

Slocum cocked a brow, but said nothing.

"Course, we're used to things like that," she went on. "Havin' a couple of big, tough galoots in the house at the same time, I mean. We got our ways of keepin' 'em apart. Got to. Last time we mingled the wrong sorts of men, my house got burned down. Don't want to trouble you with the details, though."

It was just as well. Slocum nodded. "I reckon you're smart, Mandy. Kind of like a preemptive self-defense maneuver."

It was her turn to cock a brow. "One'a them military terms I ain't supposed to understand?"

' Slocum grinned. "I reckon. Mandy, you remember what time he cut out of here?"

She nodded her blond head. She was using peroxide these days, if Slocum was any judge. "Just before you did. Maybe fifteen minutes earlier."

According to Slocum's recollection, he'd left at about a quarter to eight and headed southwest, out of town. In order for Josh to get his and Mitcham's tracks jumbled up, Mitcham must have left by the same route. Just a little earlier, that was all. Or maybe a little later, if he went to have breakfast or stock up on supplies.

"He take the southwest road out of town?" he asked, just to be on the safe side.

Mandy shrugged those little shoulders of hers. "Can't help you there, Slocum. Kept his horse up to the livery. He might have stuck around half the day, for all I know."

"The gal that was with him. She say if he said anything? About where he was headin' off to, I mean?" Slocum asked.

"Just a minute," Mandy said. She stood up and went to the door. "Becky Sue?" she called. "Can you come in here for a minute?"

A pretty face with a mop of light brown curls appeared in the doorway. She looked down at Mandy and said, all polite-like, "Ma'am?"

"Come in, honey, come in," Mandy said, and led her to the table.

Slocum liked the rest of her, too, once he got a look. Becky Sue was kind of a tall gal, with long, coltish legs, a small, high bust and a heart-shaped face. She was dressed in a pink negligee, all feathered at its plunging neckline and cuffs, and she winked at Slocum when she sat down.

Mandy poured her a cup of coffee. She took a sip and said, "Slow night, ain't it?" But she eyed Slocum up and down. It was obvious she liked what she saw, too.

Mandy asked if she remembered a particular fellow from about five nights back, who might have called himself Mitcham. "Tallish, dark, scar on his face?"

A visible shudder went through the girl. "Like I could forget him!" she spat, suddenly enraged. "That son of a bitch made me . . . Well, I don't want to say. But if he ever comes through here again, I ain't goin' nowhere with him', let alone upstairs. The pig!"

Suddenly, Slocum wanted to make it up to her in the worst kind of way.

"Did he say anything?" Mandy went on. " 'Bout where he was goin'?"

Becky Sue thought a moment, her pretty brow furrowing slightly. "Believe he said as how he was goin' down to the border, around Nogales. Said he had a job there. Didn't say what, though. Why? Is it important?"

Mandy looked over at Slocum.

"No, honey," he said to Becky Sue. "You been a big help. Thanks."

Becky Sue stood up. "You done with me, Miss Mandy?"

Slocum grinned. "She is, Becky Sue, but I ain't. That is, if you're free."

The girl smiled. She had straight, white teeth and a pretty grin, with dimples in her cheeks. She said, "I got the time, if that's what you mean."

Mandy laughed. "Well trained, that one. Go ahead, Becky Sue, if you got the inclination."

Becky Sue grinned and dipped at the knee slightly in a little curtsy. "Thanks. I do, and I will. What'd you say your name was, cowboy?"

"Slocum, baby. Just call me Slocum," he said, and got to his feet, rounded the table and took her arm.

When they walked out into the front parlor, Josh was nowhere to be seen. Neither was that little red-headed gal.

Slocum smiled a tad wider. He hoped Josh was having himself a real good time. He also hoped that Josh was already out of that bathtub and into a bed, because he wanted next dibs on some hot water.

And some female back scrubbing.

He didn't know where Josh had gone off to, and by the time Becky Sue had refilled the tub with hot water, he didn't care. Mostly because she took off that pink negligee before she did it.

All she had on underneath was a silky, skimpy pair of underpants and a camisole so thin that he could see right through it.

He was out of his clothes in no time flat, and took her in his arms. But Becky Sue was having none of it. Playfully, she shoved at his chest and said, "Just you hold on there, Slocum. I think you need a little scrubbing before we get to anything serious."

Her hand went to his face, skittering over his three days of stubble as if it were sandpaper. "Hmmm," she said, and clucked her tongue disapprovingly. "A good shave, too."

Slocum tried to will his erection down to a tolerable level—not exactly an easy thing—and stepped into the tub.

The water was just right, and he sank down in it immediately. Becky was right behind him with a razor, a towel and a pot of shaving soap. She set them down on a little footstool, knelt on the floor right beside the tub, then stripped off her camisole.

"Wouldn't want to get it all wet and soapy, now would I?" she asked.

"No, ma'am," he answered with a big grin.

Then she stood up on her knees and proceeded to lather his whiskers.

She bent over him as she worked, her tight, little bosoms moving with her body, and he reached up for them, began to stroke them, play with them. The nipples, already tight, tightened even more until they stuck out, long and hard and deep pink as pencil erasers.

She took a deep breath, giggled softly and whispered, "Now, don't you be gettin' me all stirred up, Slocum, or you might just accidentally lose an ear." She brushed a kiss over the tip of his nose, and before he could tilt his head far enough to catch her lips with his, she had pulled back and was wiping the razor again.

She made a clucking sound, shook her head and said, "Now, just you be patient. I'm almost done."

"You're about to finish me, all right, girl," he said with a grin, and made a new grab for her breast.

She let him have his way with it while she completed the last few strokes on his throat, and then she washed off the last of the soap. By this time, Slocum was about as hot as a fireplace poker and working his way toward a branding iron.

But she pulled away from him again, and this time, she stood all the way up. Regarding him thoughtfully, she put a finger to her chin and said, "Now I suppose you ought to have a real good bath. You've soaked enough to loosen up the first layer, anyhow."

And she stepped out of those silky little underpants in one smooth move.

The next thing he knew, she was lowering herself into the bathwater, too, reaching beneath her to find his hard cock under the soapy water, and easing herself right down on it. She must have been a whole lot more ready than she appeared, because she was as slippery wet as if she'd been buttered.

Slocum was about to take her into his arms and start to pump for all he was worth, but again, she put her hand on his chest. There was a sponge in it.

"Just go slow, baby," she whispered. "Let me do the work."

Reluctantly, he sat back, and as he did, she gave him a little squeeze with her internal muscles.

It just about shot him through the ceiling.

"There, there, big boy," she teased, and began to

scrub at his shoulders and chest with the soapy sponge.

He reached out and cupped her breasts, like ripe peaches, in his hands. And as she washed him, she began to swivel her hips, slowly, lazily, around him.

Her knees were up under his armpits and he brought his legs up, so that she could rest against his thighs. And then she grew slit eyed, and when he drew her to him again, she didn't resist.

She just kept those hips slowly moving, while she began to gently squeeze him again with her internal muscles.

Slocum took her lips and kissed her deeply, letting her sigh escape into his mouth. He began to push up into her, creating a whole new series of sensations that made the hair on the back of his neck stand up. And she swirled faster, faster all the time, grinding her hips down into each of his upthrusts.

They came as one, and when they did, the water sloshed over the bathtub sides. She hunched against his chest, still impaled on his cock, and whispered, "Great day in the mornin'!"

Blowing air out through his mouth, Slocum murmured, "You can say that again, darlin'."

While Slocum was having his "bath," Josh and Lulu, the little redhead, were having a high old time. At least, Josh thought it was the best time he'd ever had. He forgot all about Slocum, even forgot all about Mitcham, when Lulu went to work.

She was soft and sweet-voiced, and reminded him a little of a gal he'd known back home, a sweet gal named Miss Elizabeth Sykes who'd got wed and moved away to California. In a way, it was a little like being with her.

He'd always wanted to be with her, so that part was nice.

Past nice, in fact.

They'd already done it two times, both of them on the bed, when Josh got an idea into his head.

"Miss Lulu?" he asked just as politely as a naked man with a naked woman can ask anything. "Would you mind if . . . That is, would it be a trouble to you if . . . What I mean, is . . . ," he stammered.

She rolled over and took his face in her hands. "What is it, you sweet thing?" she asked.

Josh blushed. Although how he could still blush after what they'd just done twice was beyond him.

He said, "Miss Lulu, would you mind if we did it again?"

She cocked her head, red curls swinging. "Course I wouldn't mind," she said with a soft chuckle. "Don't you know? That's what I'm here for, sweetie."

Josh swallowed. "I mean, would you mind if we did it . . . um . . . on that table over there?"

Lulu laughed softly, and it sounded like music to Josh. She said, "Why not, sugar? Miss Mandy says you're to have everything you want."

She slipped off the mattress and stood before him, all sleek and naked and as redheaded below as she was above. She cocked her hip and put a hand on it, then put a finger to the side of her cheek.

"So, sweetie, you want me on my back again, or on my tummy?"

Josh swallowed hard, then broke out in a big grin.

5

Come the next morning, Slocum and Josh took breakfast at the café down the street, Margie Bee's Busy Kitchen by name.

"So that's what I figure happened," Slocum said over his eggs. "Mitcham and I left the stable right within about a half hour or so of each other, and you followed the tracks. But somewhere along the way, you got onto the wrong set."

Josh nodded slowly while he chewed his sausage. "Reckon," he said, once he swallowed. "Makes sense. There was two sets about the same. Same size man, same size horse, you know? But there was one place out on the trail where they split up. I coulda showed you if we'd rode back the same way I came out. It's not very far from town, either. Damn!" he added angrily. "I flipped me a coin and everything!"

Slocum chuckled. "Well, hell, that shoulda sent you the right way."

"You're makin' fun of me." Josh pouted.

"A little," Slocum said, one corner of his mouth quirking up.

Sheepishly, Josh grinned and shrugged. "So what do we do now?"

Slocum took a sip of his coffee. It wasn't the best

or the hottest, but it was drinkable. And the hash browns were so good that they could have made up for a multitude of sins.

"I reckon that we start out all over again," Slocum said. "Those tracks are gonna be mighty faint, but there ain't been much wind, and there sure as hell ain't been no rain. Can you recollect just where those two trails split up?"

Josh nodded. "Sure can. It was right at a cross in the trail, by a big cluster of yellowish boulders—I remember, 'cause they were ringed with stains around the last foot or so, like every coyote in the country had been markin' 'em—and there were a couple of big saguaros real close."

"Good," Slocum replied around a mouthful of bacon. He swallowed, grabbed up another forkful of hash browns and, before he shoved them in his mouth, added, "Don't see any reason why we shouldn't start out as soon as we finish up our breakfast and stop by the general store for a few provisions."

"That where you get those good vegetables you cooked up that first night?" Josh asked.

"Sure was," Slocum answered around the hash browns. They were mighty good. Course, all that entertaining exercise he'd got last night might have something to do with his appetite.

Josh grinned—at the thought of those vegetables, Slocum supposed.

"I'm all for that, then," he said. Then he paused, and his face grew solemn. "Slocum?"

"Yeah?"

"I just wanna say, well, thanks for everything. For helpin' me go after that bastard, Mitcham. For fixin' up my head. And for . . . last night."

Slocum nodded, just as serious as Josh. "No problem, Josh. First off, I'm as keen to get this Mitcham as you are. I didn't say anything, but besides that deal with the Mexicans I told you about, there was a thing from a couple of years ago that I'm still pissed about."

He didn't elaborate. He just paused to take a sip of coffee. "So," he went on, "I got as much at stake as you do, almost. And as for fixin' up your scalp, well, I was sort of obligated, seeing as how it was my slug that tore it up in the first place. How's it feelin'?"

Josh looked a little embarrassed. "Itchy as sin. Still tender. But I shot you in the arm first. How's that doin'?"

"No problem," Slocum said nonchalantly, mainly because it was the truth. "You just grazed me a little. Nothin' to worry about. It's already scabbed over real good. And as for last night," he added with a grin, "I figured that with all you been through lately, you deserved it. You have yourself a good time with that little Lulu gal?"

The giant grin that suddenly stretched Josh's face was all the answer that Slocum needed.

• • •

A couple of hours later, they came to the junction in the trail near the saguaros and the big yellow rocks. Josh had been right, Slocum thought. They did look like every coyote in the country had been lifting a leg on their lower thirds for a few thousand years, because all around, the bottom foot and a half was stained about six shades darker than the rest of them.

"Well, I went straight," Slocum said, leaning on his saddlehorn. "Which way'd he go? East or west?"

Josh pointed off to the left, indicating the east.

"Funny way to get to Nogales," Slocum muttered.

"Huh?"

"That Becky Sue, last night. She said that he told her he was goin' down to Nogales. Course," Slocum added, "he coulda been lyin'. Or he could be takin' a little detour."

His saddle creaking, Slocum got down off Tubac and began to follow the trail, or at least what precious little was left of it.

There hadn't been much wind or any rain, but there'd been enough of a light breeze to blow the tracks mostly away. Also, a couple other horses, plus a few wagons had passed this way—one quite recently.

In silence, Slocum followed the trail for about ten minutes, walking along, staring at the ground, and Josh was wise enough to keep his mouth shut and let Slocum concentrate.

Finally, Slocum mounted back up. He sat there on Tubac and rolled himself a quirlie.

"Well?" said Josh, finally. "Can we follow it? Hell, I can't tell which of those prints are his. If any of 'em are."

"Oh, we can follow 'em, all right," Slocum said around his smoke, and the cupped hands holding a lucifer to it. He shook out the match, then exhaled a plume of smoke. "If it don't rain. And if he didn't do anything tricky."

"Like for instance?"

"Like leave the road and cut off through rocky territory," Slocum replied. "Any one of sixteen other things."

"Oh," said Josh, and he had the common sense to look a tad embarrassed.

Slocum clucked to Tubac and they started out at a walk, with Josh close behind. Slocum's eyes were on the ground.

Mitcham's trail was hard to follow. Sometimes it disappeared entirely, covered by the tracks of other horses or wagon wheels. But it wasn't impossible. Slocum was pretty sure he could keep his nose to it.

For a while, at least.

And frankly, he welcomed the opportunity. He hadn't been doing much of anything when he ran into Josh. Or rather, when Josh started shooting at him. He'd just finished up a good-paying job, he had plenty of money, and he was at loose ends.

Also, it was about damn time that he took care of that skunk, Mitcham.

●   ●   ●

The man who had called himself most recently Jack Mitcham had stopped next to a big tank—a naturally hollowed out depression in the rock where rainwater collected—and was washing the trail dust from his scarred and stubbled face.

Nearby, his horse was taking advantage of the breather, too, and drinking water gratefully.

Mitcham wasn't in a hurry. Oh, sure, he'd figured out that kid he'd shot back in Flagstaff, at the Bird's Eye, was following him for a bit. He shook water from his face and hair like a dog, then combed his fingers through his still greasy hair and slapped his hat back on.

He'd thought for sure that kid was dead, that he'd got all three of them with that one shot. *Damn it anyway,* he thought, running a hand over his face, skimming away the excess water and flicking off a water bug in the process.

"Damned tank bugs," he muttered.

Because the water collected, then just sat there for days or weeks until the beating sun evaporated it, tank water was always buggy as hell. Skimmer bugs, Jesus bugs, bloodworms—you name it. Sometimes tanks even held tiny little freshwater shrimps or miniature frogs or polliwogs. Mitcham would be damned and deep fried if he knew where they went when the water dried up.

The horse didn't seem to mind, though. He was still over there. Mitcham could see every gulp of water as it traveled from his lowered head and down—or up, depending on how you looked at it—his throat.

Yes, he knew about that bullheaded kid. Heard tell of him four days after the shooting, that the kid had lived through it, and was supposed to be after him. Close by, too.

And to tell the truth, it had put a jump in him. Not the kid being after him, but the fact that his slug had failed to kill all three of those idiot farmers. Hell, you'd think farmers would be soft! A slug ought to cut right though them, like a hot poker through butter. And those boys were farmers, all right.

He could tell that the slap second he saw them, despite the thin veneer of the West that had settled over them.

Well, Mitcham had his ear to the right gossips in Paso Robles, and one of them, old Arnie Sarknussen, had mentioned that the boy was over in Creole Center and headed his way, and that the boy was madder than a wet hen with her tail feathers plucked.

Mitcham had galloped fast to Paso Robles, tucked his horse in the livery, spent the night over at the whorehouse, then ridden out ahead of the usual batch of travelers in the morning. He figured that his tracks were long covered up by those of other horses and buggies and the like.

After all, he hadn't seen or heard shit about that kid since Arnie had spilled the beans, and it had been what, six days or so? Maybe seven?

Course, he hadn't talked to anybody in about four or five days, either . . .

He'd thought about just hanging around town, waiting for that farmer to ride in from Creole Center. By rights, the boy was his kill, after all. He ought to have had the sense to stay dead. But then, the sheriff in town wasn't exactly friendly, and Mitcham figured he didn't need any more trouble.

If the kid kept coming, he could always get him farther down the line somewhere. Sort of set things right.

So he'd gone to Paso Robles—and dropped that red herring about Nogales at the whorehouse—then went on his way.

Frankly, it hadn't much mattered to him if the kid caught up or not. If he did, Mitcham would kill him. If he didn't, well, the boy would probably live to bounce his grandkids on his knee.

Either way, it made no difference as far as Mitcham was concerned.

Still, he'd told that whore back in Paso Robles that he was going to Nogales. That would likely do well enough to throw the kid off the scent. Actually, he was headed for the southern New Mexico Territory, toward a little town called Cholla. A man named Vance Thane had sent for him, and he was late already.

"Well," he said, rising from his haunches and stretching his arms, "I won't have to keep an eye cocked for *that* little bastard anymore."

He ran his head around in a slow circle, listening to the bones pop as the kinks went away, then slowly, he started walking toward his horse. "That boy is long lost in the cactus."

He put a foot to leather and mounted with a groan and a creak. He gathered his reins, but before he moved the horse along, he looked back over his shoulder.

Not for the kid, but for somebody else.

He'd had the damnedest feeling lately.

You didn't live long in this profession if you weren't just a little bit clairvoyant, and lately that little voice inside was telling him that he was in danger.

Not from the kid, though. From somebody else, somebody from his past.

He put his heels to the horse and set off toward the southeast at a slow jog, accompanied by the sound of water sloshing in the horse's belly.

No, he wasn't too worried about that kid.

But somebody was out there. He could feel it.

6

Josh followed along behind Slocum silently: at least, in voice.

Soft sounds were all around, though. The creak of their saddle leather, the plod of their horses's hooves, the soft sighs of breeze through the brush, chipper or plaintive or lilting birdsong, and the occasional screech of an overhead hawk on the hunt.

The smells of dusty vegetation that normally filled his nose had lately been replaced by the stench of creosote. They were riding through a big patch of it, and somebody's wagon wheel had run off the road a bit, breaking off the brushy creosote twigs and intensifying the odor.

Slocum didn't seem to mind, though.

If anybody had ever been single-minded, it was Slocum. Josh reminded himself for the thirtieth time how fortunate he'd been that his bullet had only grazed Slocum's arm, and that Slocum had been awful forgiving about it.

More forgiving than what he deserved.

From what Miss Lulu had told him last night, Slocum had himself quite a reputation—and the stuff to back it up with, too.

Slocum's reputation was big enough, Josh thought,

that he was surprised it hadn't spread as far as Iowa! Course, mayhap it had. He just wasn't much for going to bars, where such things were talked about, when he lived back home. And he hadn't been much for dime novels. Miss Lulu had said that Slocum was in lots of those, too. Why, Josh figured he was traveling with an honest to God celebrity!

According to Lulu, Slocum was one tough hombre, as feared in a street fight or with a gun or rifle as he was longed for at every whorehouse in the West.

The man seemed to make men and women wet their britches, although for entirely different reasons.

Yes, Josh was mightily glad—not to mention thankful—that Slocum had been in a forgiving mood the day he'd found him. And that they were now on the same side, going after the same son of a weasel's butt that had killed his brothers.

Mitcham was in for a world of trouble, all right.

And if Josh lived through this, he'd have some kind of tale to tell, once he got back home.

If he got back home.

He hadn't really given much thought to that until he got Slocum on his side. He supposed he was just sort of "on the scent" and going on instinct, just going and going until he could catch up with Mitcham.

But now that he had a partner—and one who actually knew what he was doing, was famous for it, in fact—things were a little bit different.

Up ahead, Slocum stopped his horse, then dismounted. Josh rode up next to him and did the same.

"What?" he said.

Slocum was loosening his horse's girth. "Nothing. Just stopping to rest the horses."

Josh scratched his head. "They ain't done nothing faster than a walk all mornin'."

"Still need to stop and water," Slocum said. "You know better'n that." He hadn't looked toward Josh yet. He was presently concerned with pulling down his water bag and transferring liquid into a nose bag.

Josh shrugged, then eased his mount's girth, too. As he filled his horse's nose bag with water, he asked, "How are you—I mean *we*—coming? On the tracks, I mean."

Slocum finally looked his way. "Fine," he said. Josh could read nothing from his face. He supposed Slocum was famous for that, too. "Sometimes it just plain disappears, sometimes it's back, but it's always faint. He's still on this trail, though."

"But can't we go any faster?" Josh asked as he rubbed Stoney's forehead. "I mean, what if it rains, or comes up one'a them windstorms like I hear they got down here?"

"No," Slocum said curtly. He turned toward Josh and said, "I know you got a fire burnin' in your belly to catch up with Mitcham. And no, I ain't gonna say anything about how you lost him in the first place."

Josh felt his neck getting hot, but if it was as red as it felt, Slocum didn't seem to notice.

"But the thing is," Slocum went on, "if we start tearin' after him and he leaves the trail, we're gonna miss it entirely. You want to backtrack ourselves a day or two and find out his trail is altogether vanished?"

Josh felt awfully stupid. But then, this wasn't anything new for him. He said, "You're right."

Slocum put away his horse's nose bag and tightened his girth. " 'Sides," he said, "Mitcham's travelin' at a walk, pure and simple. He musta been pretty damned sure he lost you already."

Now, Josh took some umbrage at this. He pulled himself up and said, "How the heck could he know I was followin' him in the first place?"

Slocum just shrugged. "These boys have a way of knowin' it," he said. "Or just plain feelin' it. He musta figured somebody was doggin' him. Why else you think he'd leave a red herring back at the whorehouse?"

Josh cocked his head. Why was Slocum talking about fish all of a sudden? He said, "Huh?"

"A false clue," Slocum said, and stepped up into the saddle. "That thing about how he was going to Nogales. Nogales is back that way, if you don't know." He pointed off to the southwest, whereas they'd been following Mitcham toward the southeast.

Josh didn't answer. He just shook the last few drops of water from his nose bag, shoved it back down in his saddlebag, adjusted his girth and got on his horse. "All right," he said.

Slocum didn't move, though. He rested his hands on his saddlehorn and said, "Look, I know you've got a fire in your gut. I already said that. And I know you're antsy as hell to revenge your brothers. What I'm tellin' you is that if you don't know when to stay relaxed about a thing—and when to jump fast—you ain't gonna last very long out here."

Josh nodded, but said nothing. He felt that Slocum was treating him just a little too much like a kid. And furthermore, it sort of pissed him off when Slocum was always reading his mind. Or seeming to. It was spooky as all get out.

Slocum clucked to his horse, who moved out at a walk. Then Slocum called back over his shoulder, "Sorry if I make you feel like I'm treatin' you like a kid, Josh. Don't mean to. Just that everybody seems like a kid to me, these days."

Beneath his breath, Josh muttered, "God *damn* it!" and kneed his horse into a walk.

How the hell did Slocum *do* that?

Grover Detroit, all five-feet-eight of him, leaned against the bar at the Red Dog Saloon and stroked his mustache. Calmly, in a voice as melodious as it was intense, he said, "You want to run that past me again, kid?"

The floor had already cleared. Across the expanse of splintery planks, spotted here and there by an over-turned, rough-hewn chair or a random pile of wood shavings, stood a young, self-styled shootist whom Grover really didn't want to kill today.

Why, the kid couldn't be more than eighteen!

The kid spoke. He said, "I told you to draw that Peacemaker, mister."

Detroit replied, "Oh, I heard that part. You got a name? Don't like to have a gun battle with a feller lest I know his name."

"Banner," the boy spat arrogantly. "Darryl Banner. It's a name you'll remember as long as you live. Which ain't gonna be long."

"Well, Darryl Banner," Detroit said, "if I may be so bold as to ask, what makes you want to walk in here and shoot me? I don't know you from dirt. We never met before. All I want is to have a beer or two, and maybe a hand of poker. I'm a peaceable citizen. Ask any man here."

He waved a hand wide, indicating the cowering customers, none of whom knew him from spit.

" 'Cause you're Grover Detroit," the boy answered. He was tallish and redheaded, and probably still waiting for his beard to come in all the way.

"And peaceable, my ass!" Banner went on. "I heard all about you. You got a reputation. You're fast." He smiled. "But not near as fast as me."

Detroit still made no move for his gun. His right hand rested on the bartop, twirling his beer mug, leaving wet circles that soaked into the rough wood. Slowly, he shook his head.

"Now, Darryl," he said patiently. "You really want to bet your life on that?"

"I ain't bettin' nothing," the kid said.

"Your words, not mine," Detroit muttered sadly.

"Don't talk to me like you're my pa," Darryl said, a little too angrily. "Dammit, Detroit! Come on! Draw, old man! What'sa matter, Grover? Past your prime?"

Now, Grover Detroit was far too seasoned to respond to taunts, but he was beginning to think that this kid was too dumb to be talked out of anything. He had his heart—which, for the moment, was still in one healthy piece and beating—set on shooting himself a gunfighter, and Detroit just happened to be the lucky one he'd chosen for the honor.

But then Detroit thought of something.

"Your pa ordered you around a lot, did he, Darryl?" he asked quietly.

"Don't want to talk about my pa," the boy snarled. "I want you should skin that damn smokewagon of yours and quit talking like we was at a church social. Jesus! You're supposed to be a shootist!"

"I ain't your pa, that's for certain," Detroit went on, and his voice was as calm as the kid's was boiling over.

"If you're mad at him," he continued, "don't go round takin' it out on the general populace. I'm just a man tryin' to have himself a beer or two and a little peace and quiet."

"Don't you be talkin' about my pa, dammit!" Darryl half-shouted.

Wrong subject, Detroit thought with a resigned sigh. Well, it wasn't the first time.

Now the kid was really mad. His nostrils flared

with every quick breath, and his face had gone hot pink. Sometimes messing with a man's mind worked, sometimes it didn't.

In this case, it'd had exactly the opposite effect Detroit was looking for.

"Just remember, Darryl Banner, you brought this on yourself," Detroit said as he slowly turned to face the boy full on. He let his hand slide from the bar to dangle loosely at his side. "You could've had you a nice long life. Got married. Had kids. Maybe grandkids. You could have—"

"Ain't interested in *coulds* and *couldn'ts*, old man," Darryl said, his fingers literally twitching. Detroit could see the pulse in his neck beating from across the room. It was way too fast. "Just interested in right here, right now."

"You ain't going to make me draw first, Darryl," Detroit said with a sad sigh. "I won't do it."

"Chicken," the boy sneered, and suddenly went for his gun.

Detroit's slug had pierced his heart before he cleared leather. The late Darryl Banner's lead was fired harmlessly through the floor, and into God knew what was underneath it.

"Goddamn waste," Detroit said, drinking the last gulp of his beer as chairs scraped, tables were uprighted, and men slowly came out from hiding.

He holstered his Colt. "Goddamn terrible waste."

7

"Turned off," said Slocum. He reined Tubac off the south side of the trail and waited for the lagging Josh, riding the bay, to catch up with him.

This was their second day on Mitcham's track, and the trace was growing fainter and fainter. There had been one stretch of really good ground, late yesterday afternoon, where the tracks had been pretty clear and they'd been able to lope along while Mitcham's tracks kept to a jog or a walk.

That was good. Slocum figured they'd gained a little time on him.

But not enough.

Mitcham was still at least three days ahead of them, maybe four. The Lord had best cut them a break pretty soon, or they'd lose him out there.

What lay beyond the trail that passed for a road was an open expanse of brushy, brittle desert, nothing on it growing more than knee-high. No sign of water for miles. A range of hills rode the eastern horizon, but other than that, the landscape was unbroken.

"Here?" Josh said, suddenly beside him.

"Yup," Slocum replied, and stuck the smoke he'd just rolled into his mouth. He reached for a lucifer.

"You think we got enough water?" Josh asked.

Slocum lit his smoke and shook out the sulphur-tip with a quick flick of his wrist. "If we're careful." He pointed ahead, toward the low range of mountains. "There's a good-sized tank at the base of those hills."

He took a long drag on his smoke, and sent the exhaled fumes jetting out his nostrils. He was thinking that it was entirely possible they would lose the trail and go home empty-handed.

But then, he thought that if Mitcham had cut off the road just here, he might be heading for that same tank Slocum had just pointed out to Josh. He'd realized it at the second he pointed in its direction. It was a straight line from where they now sat, and the only water for miles.

As he smoked, eyes searching out over the vast plain before him, he mulled this over. There was no trace of the trail beyond ten feet from the side of the road, where the substrate changed from packed, dusty clay to the gravelly desert floor and blackened, volcanic rock.

He slid his boot from the stirrup, raised his foot and ground his quirlie out on the sole.

Josh, waiting patiently all this time, finally said, "Well? We gonna just sit here all day?"

"Nope," said Slocum, and urged Tubac forward, out onto the desert, with his head bent over and his gaze on the ground before him.

He'd been right. Mitcham's tracks faded away to sheer nothing. Even the sparse twigs and grasses the horse would have snapped off in its passing had used the three or four days since to regenerate. His trail was well disguised. Nearly erased.

Slocum swiveled back toward Josh.

"Try to keep up," he said. He turned back and sank his heels to Tubac.

Behind him, he heard Josh howl a surprised "Jesus, Slocum!" then the sound of his hoof beats, rapidly following.

They galloped across the plain, headed straight for that faraway, unseen tank in the hills.

Just outside Cholla, Mew Mexico, little more than a wide spot in the road, Latham Siler sat on the wide veranda of a stylish and very large Victorian house, complete with curlicues and completely out-of-keeping with the surrounding landscape. Absently, he dealt out poker hands on the wicker table in front of him. Before him, down in the broad valley, grazed just part of a herd of fat beef cattle.

He didn't pay them much attention.

Three of diamonds.

Queen of clubs.

Ten of hearts.

"Missah Silah?"

He looked up at the Chinese manservant who had padded out from the house so quietly that Siler hadn't heard him, not even the swinging shut of the door behind him.

"You gotta tippy-toe everywhere, you goddamn little Chink?" Siler growled.

"Tippy-toe, tippy-toe," said the man, nodding and smiling, and seemingly unaware of—or unfazed by—the insult. "Missah Thane, he wanna see you now. In house, in big room."

Siler threw down another card. Ace of spades. He said, "All right, all right. Just a minute."

"Okey dokey." The happy Chinaman nodded. "Good-good. I tell now, okay?"

"Yeah, yeah," Siler growled, but the Chinaman didn't wait for it. He was already backing silently toward the front door, bowing and smiling that same old stupid grin, his long black braid bobbing over his black pajamaed shoulder.

It beat the hell out of Latham Siler why a fellow like Vance Thane, who could have afforded to hire all the pretty Mexican señoritas he wanted to take care of his place, would hire a goddamn Chink, probably off a railroad crew.

Hell, if Siler had old man Thane's money he would have used it a whole lot differently. He wasn't quite sure how, but it wouldn't have been on this fancy house or all those cattle, no sir. Probably something more like a lot of women and great deal of good whiskey, or maybe a little travel.

He stood up, scraping back his chair, and walked down the long porch to the front door. He passed the only other shootist to arrive so far—Trey Blackfoot, who sat on the porch swing whittling, dropping thin, curled shavings of soft pine to the porch floor.

Blackfoot didn't even look up as Siler passed, letting a simple grunt suffice to acknowledge the passage of his boots.

Well, what the hell do you want him to do? Siler thought, mad at himself for being angry at Blackfoot. *Stand up and bow?*

No, he didn't want that. For one thing, Blackfoot was six-feet-five to his five-ten, and made him feel as short and dinky as a kid. For the second, Blackfoot was half-Indian—dark, coppery skin, hair in a thick braid hanging halfway down his back, and meaner looking than a javelina boar with a butt full of boils.

Blackfoot could most likely pound him into the ground with the blow of one fist.

Siler reminded himself to save up his mad for when he needed it.

He opened the front door and entered the foyer, then turned right and went into the parlor, remembering to take off his hat as he passed through the doorway. Thane was a regular bug on manners. Lord, you'd think the old man was married or something, with a bunch of daughters and a wife running round him, insisting on cleaned boots and the silverware in the right place and string ties. But no, Thane was a bachelor.

He sure was an awful picky one.

"You wanted to see me?" Siler said to the back of Vance Thane's chair. All he could see of the man was one hand, draped over the chair's arm and twirling a half-filled brandy glass.

Slowly, Vance Thane stood up. He was a big man,

about six-feet-two, and nearly as wide as he was tall. There wasn't one jovial thing about him.

Not that Siler minded much. He was in it for the money, pure and simple. He didn't care who paid him, so long as they did.

"Yessir, Mr. Siler," Thane said. As always, that light, airy, tenor voice coming out of such a big man came as a surprise. Thane gestured toward the small bar in the corner. "Brandy?"

"No, thank you, sir," Siler said politely, hat working in his fingers. His tastes ran more toward bourbon and branch.

"Ah," said Thane, as if Siler's refusal of a brandy disclosed mountains of information to him. "To business, then."

"Yessir."

"As you know," Thane said, walking heavily to the window, "I hired three crack shootists for this particular job. I am still waiting for the third." He stopped, the sun lighting his face and chins, glinting off his oiled and slicked salt-and-pepper hair and illuminating what was left of the brandy in his glass. It glowed, jewel-like.

"Yessir." It wasn't that Siler was all that anxious to get to work. In fact, Thane's third man could take all week if he wanted.

Siler was enjoying taking it easy, with a roof over his head that he didn't have to pay for. That crazy little Chinaman cooked pretty good for a Chink, and

Thane had a fair supply of real Kentucky bourbon in that little corner bar of his.

Siler didn't think Thane had figured out that he'd discovered it as yet. He'd never seen Thane drink anything but brandy.

"I have decided to give him another forty-eight hours," Thane continued. He was staring out the window rather intently. Siler couldn't see what he was looking at, but it had to be pretty interesting to catch his eye like that. "If he hasn't turned up in that span of time, then you and Mr. Blackfoot will handle this business alone."

That didn't sound like such a good idea to Siler, but he nodded and repeated, "Yessir."

Anything to keep the old man happy and the Kentucky bourbon flowing.

"That's all, Mr. Siler," Thane pronounced. The son of a bitch hadn't looked at him but the once. He was still staring out the window, although now in a different direction.

Corking his irritation, Siler said, "You want I should pass this along to Blackfoot?"

He wasn't surprised when Thane said, "I would appreciate it, Mr. Siler."

Thane had shown a marked distaste for anything having to do with Blackfoot ever since the half-breed rode in two days ago. Of course, he didn't seem to cotton much to Siler, either, but at least he talked to him. Siler had been conveying messages from Thane to Blackfoot ever since.

Siler nodded and risked a longing glance at the bar. He normally waited for Thane to go to bed before he began sneaking bourbon. Good thing Thane turned in early.

"I'll tell him," Siler said, once he realized his nod had gone unnoticed.

"Very good," said the fat man, turning from the window and walking ponderously back to his chair without even a glance in Siler's direction. "You may leave now, Mr. Siler."

"Yessir" once again issued from Siler's mouth. He was sort of half-wishing somebody'd hire him to take out Thane. Being treated lower than a cur dog got on a man's nerves after a while. Somebody ought to remind Thane that he'd hired Siler all the way from Missouri—and Blackfoot, too, all the way from Texas, he supposed, grudgingly—because they were the best around.

And that a man like Thane, who probably couldn't run more than three or four steps without his lungs giving out, who likely hadn't picked up a gun in five or ten years, and who had gone soft on brandy and cigars and catered dinners and fat beef roasts, still did have a few things he needed to be afraid of.

Money couldn't buy your life if somebody was set on taking it.

Siler backed out of the parlor, through the open pocket doors, and into the front hall, where he slapped his hat on his head again.

Well, money was money. And Thane was paying pretty good.

The screen banged behind him when he exited the house, and he walked back down the porch to the Chink's calls of "No bang screen! No bang screen! Missah Thane, he no like!"

Siler ignored his yammering and stopped beside Blackfoot, casting his shadow over the half-breed's hands, and the wood in it. It looked to him like Blackfoot was carving a thick chain made out of wood. Three links of a chain, anyhow.

Blackfoot looked up.

Now, Blackfoot was out of Texas, and he was one ugly son of a bitch. His disconcertingly light gray eyes were too close together, for one thing, and he had a long, thin face and nose, like a hatchet sitting on an axe blade. His beard and mustache were sparse as a kid's, and grew in long wiry wisps from his jaw and the outside corners of his upper lip.

"Thane says we're gonna wait two days for that third gun he hired," Siler said. "If he don't show up by then, it's just you and me."

Blackfoot grunted, shook his head, then went back to his whittling.

Siler snorted softly, then walked on, down to his end of the porch.

He figured that this was about the least sociable bunch of folks he'd been around in a long time. Hell, he usually got on better than this with folks he was about to kill.

He slumped down in his chair again and picked up his cards, then shuffled them. Thane hadn't even told them just who this other gun was. Must not be so big or famous as himself or Blackfoot, if Thane was willing to start without him.

Course, Thane might just have a bee in his goddamned bonnet. Probably didn't matter to him whether Siler and Blackfoot lived or died.

Which was about the way Siler felt about the whole deal.

He began to deal out cards once again.

Seven of spades.

Three of hearts.

Nine of clubs . . .

8

"There it is," Slocum said, pointing.

Josh stood in his stirrups. A big, relieved grin spread over his face. "I'm mighty glad to see it," he said.

"Might change your mind about that, once we get up real close," Slocum muttered, and dug his heels into Tubac's sides.

All he heard from Josh was a muffled "Huh?"

At a lope, it only took a couple of minutes to reach the tank. Slocum slid off Tubac, who wasn't even slightly winded, and allowed him to drink. Then he lay down on his belly at the water's edge, skimmed the bugs away to make a clear spot, and put his lips to it.

The water was warm and slightly bitter, but it did the job of slaking his thirst. By the time he stood up to get his water bag, Josh was down on his belly and drinking.

"Careful of the bugs," Slocum said as he opened the neck of the bag and squatted to fill it.

Josh didn't answer him. Too busy drinking, Slocum thought with a grin. Just wait until the time he had to go two or three days without water, instead of one measly afternoon!

He glanced over again. Josh had his water bag down, and was kneeling at the edge of the tank, trying to fill the bag without getting too many of the water bugs.

"Just hold the whole thing under," Slocum said, and indicated his. "Like this. You can get the bugs out later."

He pulled his filled bag from the tank and sat there a couple of seconds, holding the neck wide. Then, after all the insects had floated to the surface, he lowered the neck slightly, allowing the top two inches of water to flow out. Along with the wildlife.

"See?" he said.

"Right," replied Josh with a nod. He pulled his bag from the water and sat there with it, its neck spread. "Sure tastes nasty, don't it? Not that I mind. Still water, and it's still wet."

"That it is." Slocum rose, tied his water bag back in place, then took down his two canteens and squatted again.

"How much time you think we gained on him?" Josh asked.

"A day, maybe," Slocum said. "Maybe more, maybe less."

"Hope it's more," Josh muttered.

"Now we just gotta figure where he went from here," Slocum said as he recapped his canteens. He slung their straps over his saddle horn, then eased Tubac's girth. The horse hadn't been hot when they rode in, Slocum having paced their journey from the road to here, but he deserved a break.

Slocum could use a little out-of-the-saddle time, too. He unbuckled his left saddlebag and rooted around for a piece of jerky to gnaw on.

Josh didn't need to be told to do the same. Slocum watched as he, too, loosed his gelding's girth. He walked over to the rocks, scraped his boot around to check for scorpions, thumbed back his hat, then sat down in the purple shade of a tall boulder. There was a piece of jerky in his hand.

"How long?" asked Josh from the shade. "Before we move again, I mean."

"Fifteen, twenty minutes," replied Slocum. "We've got a couple hours' travel time before we have to camp for the night." He squinted off into the distance.

"Yeah," said Josh, chewing on his goat meat. "But which direction?"

"Good question," said Slocum. "I'm gonna do a little reconnoitering."

He set out on foot, leaving Josh and the horses behind. He wasn't over-fond of walking, but sometimes it did a man good to get down off his horse for a little spell. He headed out in the direction they'd been traveling.

Josh hollered after him, but he called back, "Just stay sat."

It took him exactly seventeen minutes to find the track. It was there, just barely. Beyond the rocks, the ground turned to more loose gravel, but it was mixed with clay that still held a hint of a track in its dry and dusty surface. It looked to Slocum like Mitcham was headed for the first pass to the east.

He walked back to the tank, and found Josh drowsing in the shade, that chunk of jerky still in his hand, half-eaten.

He nudged the kid with his boot. "Rise and shine," he said. "Time to go."

Josh blinked a couple of times, then shot to his feet. And Slocum thought that it must be pretty damned nice to be so young and limber. The kid probably didn't even appreciate it. You never did, when you were young.

They collected their mounts and climbed into the saddles again, and Slocum pointed out Mitcham's track.

He nodded toward the distant pass.

"That don't look too far," Josh observed.

"Far enough. We won't make it tonight," Slocum replied. "Distance can fool you out here."

Josh just shrugged.

Slocum led the way, at a slow jog.

Grover Detroit had just stepped down off his mare, Kitty, and was preparing to water her. He figured that he had maybe two hours left to travel today, and then he could make camp.

For just a moment, he wished that he had a traveling companion. It got lonely out here when a man was by himself, and increasingly lonely through the years. Seemed like the only people he talked to lately had been sheriffs telling him to get out of town, or quick-tempered kids, like Whatshisname back there, trying for a reputation.

Well, rest in peace.

Kitty, a dapple gray with a roached mane, drank her water from the nose bag when he offered it. The mare wasn't so polite as her name might imply. She kicked, and she also bit Detroit every chance she got. So he was careful, as he held the water, to keep his hands and fingers clear of her mouth.

He had ceased to get mad at her when she bit him. She was a good horse otherwise, and besides, it was kind of like those were love bites she was giving him all the time.

Well, except for that time she bit him in the ass. Jesus, he couldn't sit down for a couple of days after that. The bruise, once he got a chance to look at it, was as big as a pie plate. He didn't know why Kitty had done that. Maybe she hadn't liked the livery he was putting her up in.

Lately, Detroit and Kitty had been heading south.

He wasn't quite sure why.

But it wasn't like he had any specific place to go. He had no jobs waiting, no one wanting to see him, and no one he wanted to see. No one anywhere.

The nose bag drained, Detroit shook the last couple of drops from it, then folded it and stuck it away in his saddlebag. Kitty made a grab for his sleeve, but he expertly—and without looking at her—lifted his forearm so that she caught it against her nose instead of between her teeth.

Detroit figured he knew most of her tricks by this time.

She shook her head as he mounted up and pulled a pipe from his pocket. He tamped the tobacco, then lit it and puffed. Although he wasn't sure why he was being drawn south, he didn't have anything better to do. Besides, he had this kind of jumpy feeling in the pit of his stomach, like something was about to happen. It wasn't imminent, but it was coming.

It didn't matter whether it was good or bad. Not to Grover Detroit. If something happened, well, something happened.

And it would sure as hell break the monotony.

He nudged Kitty with his knees, and she grudgingly moved out at a walk.

Jack Mitcham had been a lot of people in his lifetime. He'd come into the world as Casper Horst Vandermullen, the son of immigrant farmers in Pennsylvania.

At the age of nineteen—after an "unfortunate incident," during which he killed a man by feeding him through a threshing machine—he fled Pennsylvania and left Casper Horst Vandermullen behind, and his family to bear the shame of what he'd done.

He felt no shame whatsoever. The son of a bitch had deserved it.

He became Joe Muller for a while, then Tim Masters, then Van Horst, and on and on. Even he had forgotten a few of the somebodies he'd been.

He figured to shed Jack Mitcham after this next job. He'd snatch a new name out of the air, be someone else, start over again. Hell, maybe he'd try to settle down again.

Course, that hadn't worked so hot the last couple of times he'd tried it. He had a wife up in Wyoming he'd married while he was Tom Connors, and another in Idaho he'd married a few years before, when he was Mark Ingersoll.

Sometimes he thought about them, while he was riding along.

But most of the time, he didn't.

Waste of time, really. He couldn't even remember the first one's Christian name. This was mostly because he had only called her "Bitch" during their short marital life. As in "Where's supper, Bitch?" or "Shut up, Bitch," or "Get your fat ass over here and lift them skirts, Bitch." He did remember that he'd married her when he was practically dead drunk, and that she'd sure looked a whole lot uglier the next morning, after his head cleared. But she had a license in her hand, and the Justice of the Peace was her uncle.

He cut out of that backwater joint the first chance he got.

And he put a slug into her stinking Justice of the Peace uncle on his way out of town.

Right after, he'd changed his name to Butch

Becker. Or maybe it was Bill Holling he'd changed it to. Not that it mattered any.

At this moment, he was riding down on the flat again after crossing that low range of hills, and he figured that he'd more or less crossed over into New Mexico by now. Tomorrow he'd likely hit the town of Cholla, and he could check out this Vance Thane fellow who'd sent for him.

The sun was setting. He found himself a good place to camp, with a couple of scrubby trees to tether the horse to and some firewood scattered around. He'd still have to drink that bug-ridden water he'd brought from the tank, but there were certainly worse things. Plus, the coffee would likely cover the bitter taste.

But as he made his fire and tended his horse and set his coffee on to boil, the back of his neck began to itch more and more incessantly.

He craned his head back toward the darkening hills, but could see no one: no light, no out-of-place shadow, nothing.

Somebody was back there, though, and they were getting closer all the time. He knew it.

He just wished he knew who the hell it was.

Marcus O'Brien sat on his front porch, looking out over his flock. They were grazing not far from the house. At least, a small portion of them were. If he squinted, he could just make out Julio, he thought, and a couple of the dogs.

Things had surely changed since he first came to

Cholla. The ranchers had given him fits, certainly, and he'd even been barred—at gunpoint—from going to town for supplies.

But gradually, things had changed. Most of the cattlemen around Cholla had managed to figure out that sheep and cattle could graze the same land without hurting it in any way, shape or form. And now, after almost ten years, he was a respected member of the community.

He'd gone from sleeping on the ground with his dogs and his sheep to sleeping in a little shack he'd built. And finally, he'd built himself a house.

It was a fairly grand house, too. Oh, not so grand as Vance Thane's. But then, whose was? O'Brien's just had one story, with a nice, comfortable parlor, a kitchen, a dining room and three roomy bedrooms in case he had company, which he did from time to time.

Marcus O'Brien leaned back in his rocker and put his feet up on the porch rail. Funny old coot, that Vance Thane. Never came into town. Rarely saw people. Rumor had it that he was still vitriolically opposed to sheep men, though. He still wanted the whole range all to himself and his cattle.

Most of the other ranchers had gone over to sheep, which were thriftier, brought higher meat prices on less feed, produced wool for years before going to slaughter, and thrived on the weedy, brushy terrain. In fact, they'd eat weeds that cattle turned up their noses at.

So the ranchers had gradually switched. Either that, or combined sheep with cattle.

But Thane, he was of the old school, O'Brien thought as he puffed on his Meerschaum. He supposed that nothing could convince Thane, ever. Except maybe dying.

O'Brien shook his head sadly. Shame about Thane. There must be something wrong with the man, either physically or mentally, for him to shun the town the way he did and live out there all alone with no company, except for a Chinese servant. Even his ranch hands said they rarely ever saw him.

O'Brien's attention once again returned to his sheep, and he smiled. They were hellishly stupid, it was true. But there was something about a sheep, something you didn't get with cattle. He hesitated to even think the word, but they were, well, cute. Now, calves were cute, he supposed, but he could never see anything fetching about a steer or a cow or a bull.

Cuddly, they weren't.

O'Brien had four drovers working for him, and they and the dogs could handle far more sheep than cows. Grand dogs, he had! Arizona shepherds—or California shepherds, or Australian shepherds, depending on who you talked to. There were six of them, and they usually worked in pairs.

Four of the shaggy beasts had been born without tails, and the other two had funny little half-tails, all twisted and bent, which they wagged twenty-four hours a day, nonstop. He had three black and tan and white ones, two blue merles and one red merle, Rowdy Junior, called RJ for short.

Most cattlemen didn't care for dogs around their stock, except perhaps when they were loading them through chutes and such. O'Brien had seen three of his own dogs killed when he first came out here. Ranchers had done it, and Thane's men were responsible for two of the killings. The other, his old, original Rowdy dog, had been shot by a smaller rancher, who had since apologized, and who how had sheep himself.

O'Brien was fairly certain that letting the ranchers watch the dogs work had been part of his best publicity.

As he watched, RJ made a long run out for some stragglers. O'Brien could barely hear Julio's whistled commands, carried on the light wind. RJ stopped and lay down, and one of the tricolors—probably Rex—came around to the other side and waited for another command.

And O'Brien, smoking his pipe, was thinking what wonderful creatures they were, his dogs, and how obedient.

How calm this life had become. How calm and peaceful.

9

About four hours after they rose and started out on the trail again—sometimes loping, sometimes jogging, but always moving—Josh and Slocum found where Mitcham had camped.

Slocum, now crouched on the ground, was thoughtfully scraping a stick through the leavings of Mitcham's fire. Josh observed from the saddle.

"How long, you reckon?" Josh finally asked, since Slocum had now risen and was staring off into the distance. "Since he camped here, I mean? Two days? Three?"

Without turning to face him, Slocum said, "Last night."

Josh's mouth fell open, and he closed it with an audible snap. He swallowed hard and said, "You're joshin' me! You mean we almost caught up with the murderin' rat bastard?"

Slocum turned around and stepped back up on Tubac. "I don't fool around about stuff like that, Josh," he said. "I figure he's four, maybe four and a half hours ahead. That long gallop we did over the plain gained us a good bit of time."

"Plus shortcuttin' to the pass yesterday," Josh added. "Where you think he's headed, anyhow? This place just looks like twenty miles of nothin' in every direction."

Slocum nodded. "Yup," he said. "Closest towns are Rio Blanco, over that way . . ." He pointed due east. "And Cholla, down that way." His arm swung to the south. "My money's on Cholla. Tracks seem to lead off that way."

Now that they'd nearly caught up with Mitcham, Josh wasn't quite certain how he felt about it. Sure, he'd been full of fire and piss and righteous indignation when he caught up with Mitcham the first time. Except it had turned out to be Slocum.

Now, days later, he'd had a lot more time to think about it. He didn't know that he was feeling so brave anymore.

Last night, he had actually dreamt that he snuck out of camp in the middle of the night and had gone back to Iowa, where everything was green and the folks were friendly and you didn't have to eat jerked beef or dried goat meat all the time, and where a man could go his whole life without handling anything more serious than some hothead shouting at him at the grange meeting on Friday nights.

He'd dreamt that he was out working the fields with his shirt off, and his mama was alive again, and bringing him a tall glass of lemonade. His brothers were down at the barn, and his pa was over in the north forty, looking for a strayed shoat.

The sky was a soft, pretty blue—not bleached white, like here—and there were big, fluffy, slowly drifting clouds in the sky. Jip, good old Jip, was by his side, sticking to him like a shadow but always on the alert for any stock that needed herding or rounding up. Why, just dreaming about that dog nearly set him into crying.

Last night, that dream was the best one he'd had in a long time.

And now they were only four hours away from Mitcham. Maybe four hours away from their deaths. Suddenly, Josh wasn't so sure he wanted to go on.

He wasn't sure at all.

"Josh?" someone said, verbally shaking him from his reverie. It was Slocum, of course.

"Sorry," Josh replied, and his voice broke. "Daydream, I guess." He felt heat creeping slowly up his neck.

"Must have been a good one," Slocum said as he urged his horse into a slow jog. When Josh managed to catch up, Slocum added, "That, or a real bad one. I hollered at you three times. You were just about shakin' yourself out of the saddle, son."

At right about noon, about an hour after Slocum and Josh found his campsite, the man called Jack Mitcham rode down the main street of Cholla, New Mexico.

So far as he could see, it wasn't much of a town. Just a main street running north and south, a parallel street to Main, aptly called East First, and several cross streets with names like Cactus and Prairie and Hopi.

Most of the businesses seemed to be on Main, though. He whoaed his horse at the hitching rail in front of the Lucky Cuss saloon, stepped down, twirled his reins over the rail and went through the batwing doors.

There wasn't much business, which was just fine by him. "Beer," he said to the bartender, who had a rather impressive waxed mustache. He was, at that moment, sweeping up the floor at the far end of the room.

The barkeep set aside his dustpan, stepped back behind the bar, and in no time Mitcham had his beer. It dripped fresh foam all over the bar top. He didn't even look at it. He wanted more than that.

"Know a fella name of Thane?" he asked casually, as he lifted his mug. He took a sip, then a long gulp. He hadn't had any water but that crud he'd picked up at the tank, and the beer tasted better than fine to him.

"Supposed to live around here someplace," he added before he took a second long drink.

The bartender shrugged. "Sure," he said. He picked up a rag and absently started polishing a glass. "Everybody knows Mr. Thane. Least, they know of him. He don't come to town."

Mitcham cocked a brow. "Not ever?"

"Not that I remember," the bartender said, his eyes on the glass in his rag. "Hey, Foley!" he shouted toward a table at the rear. "You ever seen Thane?"

Foley lifted his shaggy, gray head from the newspaper he'd been reading and peered over his glasses. "Who?" he replied.

"Vance Thane," repeated the bartender. "You ever seen him?"

Foley, a middle-aged man of moderate size, scrunched his features as if giving the matter great consideration. "Yup," he finally said. "Twice. Once from a distance, once close up." His head disappeared behind the newspaper again.

Mitcham grunted, then turned back toward the bartender again. "Gabby, ain't he?"

"Yup," said the bartender, holding the shot glass up to the light. Apparently, it was polished well enough to suit him, because he set it down in the tray and picked up another. He commenced to polish it.

Mitcham was a little pissed off by these boys and their attitude, but he decided to stay calm. No sense in plugging two men when he didn't have something to prove. Also, it was a waste of ammunition.

"Don't suppose you know how to find his place," he said. "Heard it was around here somewhere."

"Yup," repeated the bartender. "Reckon everybody round these parts knows where Thane's place is."

Just when Mitcham was sure he was going to have to pull his gun to get this lummox to tell him just exactly where it was, the bartender looked up from his glass and said, "You thinkin' about hirin' on out to Vance Thane's place?"

"Maybe," said Mitcham through gritted teeth.

Fortunately, this seemed to be enough excuse for the barkeep. He put his glass down on the bar and pointed out the front window.

"What you do," he said, "is take Hopi that way. Goes about two blocks before the town peters out, but Hopi turns into kind of a road. You just follow that, and sooner or later you'll hit Thane's place. Can't miss it. It's the biggest, whale-out-of-water building you ever did see," he finished. He shook his head, as if he were disgusted by the whole idea of Thane's house.

Mitcham was about to ask just how long "sooner or later" might turn out to be, but then, he figured the answer would be "depends on how fast you travel." And if that was the answer he got, he was bound to shoot somebody: for sure, the man on the other side of the bar, and possibly himself.

So he just finished his beer, paid for it and went back outside, to his waiting horse.

About a half hour after Jack Mitcham rode out of Cholla, Grover Detroit rode in. The first thing he did was stop at the livery and get Kitty settled in. It wasn't a particularly nice stable, although it seemed to be the best one in town, and she voiced her disapproval by catching his sleeve as he left her stall, and ripping the fabric at the elbow.

"Goddamn it, Kitty," he muttered. "That's the third shirt this year you ruined."

The horse gave a satisfied snort, then turned to her hay.

"Bitch," Detroit mumbled.

He flipped a coin to the hostler, saying, "I wouldn't get too close if I was you," as he walked by, and then he made a beeline for the saloon. He was drier than a cactus after a drought.

He ordered a beer at the bar, then took it over to a table, sat down and thumbed back his hat. That feeling he kept having was coming on stronger all the time. He reckoned it was time for him to just sit back, relax and wait for whatever—or whoever—it was to come to him.

After glancing over at the bar's only other patron, ensconced behind a beat-up copy of the *Cholla Gazette,* he called to the barkeep, "Hey, you got any more newspapers? Like to do some catchin' up on the world."

"Sure," the bartender said. He rummaged beneath the bar and pulled out a copy, then blew the dust from it. "Last week's," he said as he brought it over. "New edition don't come out till tomorrow."

"Fine by me," said Detroit.

"Funny," said the bartender.

"What?" asked Detroit, cocking a brow.

"Two strangers in one day," replied the barkeep. "Just funny. We don't get many strangers around here. Do we, Foley?"

The man across the room mumbled, from behind his newspaper, "Nope."

"Mind if I buy you a drink?" Detroit asked.

The bartender's face lit up. "Well, you're sure friendlier than the last one, that's for certain."

"Go pull yourself a beer, then come on back and sit down," said Detroit amiably. "Like to have a little chat with you, if you don't mind."

As the bartender went to draw himself a beer, a pretty girl wandered down the back stairs. She was freshly made up, but looked sleepy, as if she'd only risen a short time ago. Detroit immediately pegged her as the town's token soiled dove. He wondered if she got much business in a town like this.

"Hello, Al," she said to the barkeep, at last giving him a name. "Hello, Mr. Foley," she said to the man behind the paper.

Foley nodded his head and grunted, and Al said, "Afternoon, Lola. Mayhap I got a customer for you." He nodded in Detroit's direction.

Detroit was quick to wave a hand, indicating that he wasn't interested. Lola was a dark brunette with flashing, obsidian, intelligent eyes. Cute as a button, with dimples and a bowlike smile, she had a real nice figure packed into the skimpy, light pink dress.

But he had a feeling he had more pressing things to tend to at the moment than going upstairs with a pretty whore. Even if she had dimples.

He just wished he could be certain what those things he had to tend to were.

"Maybe later, Miss Lola," he said.

"Sure thing, mister," Lola said with a generous

smile and just a hint of a wink. "I'm not going anywhere." She walked back behind the bar and set herself to brewing some tea.

Al, the bartender, came to pull up a chair right
about then. He slung his feet up on another chair,
leaned back and flipped his bar rag over his shoulder.
He lifted the beer to his lips and took a long draw on
it.

"Now, that's livin'," he said as Detroit tossed a
coin onto the table. Suds dripped from each corner of
Al's handlebar mustache as he displayed obvious rel-
ish. It was clear that a beer bought by a customer was
a lot better than one stolen when nobody was looking.

"Been a long time since anybody bought me a
beer," Al said, after he belched quite loudly. "It's
warmish this time'a day, but it's still beer, ain't it?
Now, what was it you wanted to pump my noggin
about, mister?" He leaned forward slightly. "And by
the way, you know my name. What's yours?"

"Grover Detroit," he answered. He saw no reason
to keep it a secret.

The bartender nodded, but if he'd heard the name,
he gave no sign. He said, "Well, Grover Detroit, I
figure that nobody buys a barkeep his own suds lest
he wants to know somethin', do he? So, what's your
poison?"

10

The Indian, Trey Blackfoot, saw the rider coming in before anybody else did. Down the porch, he rose from his perpetual whittling and squinted off toward the road to town long before Latham Siler made out the first speck of a rider.

He must have one hell of a pair of eyes, Siler thought.

As they watched, the speck grew into a recognizable form—although not individually recognizable to Siler. The form lazily lifted a hand in a halfway friendly greeting, and rode on up to the house. He tethered his mount at the rail, then mounted the steps.

"Howdy, boys," he said gruffly. He was a tall man, dark complected, sunburnt and rugged looking. His face, which hadn't seen a razor for a few days, also had a curious scar that ran down one side, from above the eyebrow and down over the cheek.

Saber blade, maybe, Siler thought.

The new man ignored Siler entirely, but turned to the Indian and grunted out, "Blackfoot. Long time. Fort Lea, wasn't it?"

The Indian nodded. "Hastings," he said tersely.

"Mitcham now," the newcomer replied. "Been a few things since then, but it's Jack Mitcham now."

"Fair enough," Blackfoot said. He sat back down and picked up his whittling knife again. "I'm always Blackfoot."

Siler was thinking that he was stuck out here with a couple of conversational geniuses—Mr. Goddamn Stoic Indian and Mr. Change-My-Name-Every-Couple-of-Years—when Mitcham turned toward him and offered his hand. Siler took it out of reflex.

"Mitcham," the man said.

"Siler," Siler answered, feeling like a dolt because he hadn't come up with something more interesting to say. He added, "Latham Siler," as if he hoped it would add some conversational interest to the proceedings.

Hands shaken, both men dropped their arms to their sides. "This Thane character around?" Mitcham asked.

"Yup," Siler replied. "Inside. We was about to give up on you."

When Mitcham just stared at him, he added, "Well, you're late, you know. Me and the Indian, we been here three, four days."

Mitcham didn't respond, other than to scowl slightly and say, "Front door down this way?" He hiked a thumb down toward the far end of the porch.

"Yeah," said Siler. He dropped back down into his chair and picked up his pack of cards. He could tell right off that this fellow wasn't going to be any fun at all. Why couldn't he get hired on someplace where somebody was at least talkative?

Mitcham didn't thank him. Of course, Siler didn't expect him to. Mitcham simply turned on his heel and strode off in the Indian's direction, then past him to the front door and knocked. Siler thought he must have muttered something to Blackfoot, because Blackfoot nodded.

Siler scowled. They'd better not be talking about him behind his back, that was all he had to say. And then he slumped in his chair.

Batty, he thought. *This way of livin' is makin' me plumb bats!*

He heard the screen bang as it closed behind Mitcham, and then a high-pitched stream of Chink talk as the servant scolded Mitcham.

Siler shuffled the cards. "Ain't just me, either," he muttered as he began to deal out poker hands, face up. "We're all as nutty as a buncha goddamn fruitcakes."

Grover Detroit was smoking his pipe and nursing his third beer in as many hours when the little saloon finally got an influx of new customers.

For a second, he couldn't make them out with the sun so bright behind them, but once they stepped out of the glare, he knew them, all right.

One of them, anyway.

For a second, he couldn't believe his eyes and blinked quick a few times, just to make sure it wasn't the lousy beer he'd been drinking, playing tricks on him.

It wasn't, because the man was looking right back at him.

"Grover Detroit?" the big man said, expressionless.

"Slocum?" Detroit replied, rising to his feet, his chair scraping out behind him.

The youngster that had come in with Slocum looked back and forth between the two men, as if he were puzzled and a little nervous. Even Mr. Foley, who had only moved once during the three long hours Detroit had been sitting there, biding his time and sipping on his suds, lowered his newspaper and peered over its top rim.

From behind the bar, there came the unmistakable sound of a shotgun cocking.

Al, the bartender, quietly said, "I don't want no trouble, gents. But that don't mean I ain't got a Greener under the bar, aimed your way."

One corner of Slocum's mouth quirked up into a smile. He said, "You got so you always greet your friends like this, Grover?"

Detroit said, "Ease off, Al. This big ol' galoot looks like he'll exterminate anything what crosses his path, but it's only more like fifty percent."

As he heard the sound of Al taking the shotgun off the ready, he walked out from behind the table, hand out. "Well, if you ain't a sight for these sore old eyes, Slocum!"

Slocum took his hand and slapped him hard on the back, all at the same time. "How long's it been?" he asked with a laugh. "I'll be a son of a bitch!"

"Thought you already were," said Detroit, still reeling from that back slap. Slocum was still big and still tough, and still didn't know his own strength. "Sit down, sit down," Detroit said, and gestured, pipe in hand, to the table where his beer and his folded newspaper waited. He walked back to his chair. "What the hell brings you out this way? And who's your friend?"

The boy leaned across the table and stuck out his hand, which Detroit took. The boy had a good, firm handshake and didn't pound him on the back. Detroit liked him right off the bat.

"Quaid, Mr. Detroit," he said. "Josh Quaid. Pleased to meet any friend of Slocum's."

"Then you're a smart young man, Josh," Detroit said as they each scraped out a chair. He lifted a hand and waved it until he caught Al's attention, which took all of a half a second.

"Beers all around, Al," Detroit called. He wanted to get the civilities out of the way and get down to business: Just why in the hell had Slocum come to this particular saloon in this particular town at this particular time?

Right now, all Detroit knew was that something had been vaguely drawing him here over the past few days. He wanted to know the reason why.

And he figured he'd best find out before that cutesy-pie, Lola, wandered back in and Slocum got an eyeful of her.

After all, he thought wryly, he remembered Amarillo.

"Killing sheep?" Mitcham thundered. "You called me all the way out here to kill some goddamn sheep?"

The wide expanse of Vance Thane's facial expression didn't change one whit. "For a start, Mr. Mitcham, for a start. I take it, then, that you consider vermin removal beneath you?"

"You're damn right, I do," Mitcham said vitriolically. "You could hire any idiot with a rock to kill sheep."

He nearly added *you fat lunatic,* but the promise had been five hundred dollars, and some part of him— a part back behind the shouting and indignation— figured that there had to be more to it than that. So he withheld those last three words.

But sheep!

Christ on an ever-lovin' crutch!

Thane's round face still showed nothing at all. Not displeasure, not irritation, nothing.

He spoke. "As I said, Mr. Mitcham, that will be the start of it. I would not have hired you, Mr. Blackfoot and Mr. Siler had I thought a few sheep would be the end of it."

Thane paused to pour brandy into his glass. He hadn't invited Mitcham to partake, an obvious signal of class barrier that Mitcham had been quick to pick up on. *Me boss, you servant:* that was the subtext of what Thane was saying.

Fine. Just as long as he paid what he'd promised.

And Mitcham got to shoot something besides smelly-ass sheep.

"A range war has been brewing here for some time, Mr. Mitcham," Thane continued at last. He wasn't looking at Mitcham, but out the window. "Brewing and simmering and bubbling quietly. I had thought that the ranchers would come back around to a more correct way of thinking if given enough time."

He turned his bulk to face Mitcham. "But it has become apparent that I was incorrect in this matter."

Nice way of sayin' you were wrong without sayin' it, Mitcham thought snidely.

"You gentlemen have been called here to right this grievous wrong," Thane continued, "and to put back into place the intrinsic laws of nature."

Mitcham wasn't quite sure what intrinsic meant—and frankly, he didn't much care—but he nodded like he did. "And just what's all this gonna involve?" he asked. "From me, I mean. I wanna know what I'm in for."

Thane cocked a brow, his first indication of any expression. "You're the first to ask that question," he said before he fell silent.

After a minute of listening to the Chinaman banging around in the kitchen and his own stomach growling, Mitcham broke the silence. "Well? Are you gonna answer it?"

"Yes," Thane said. "I believe that I will." He

pointed to one of a pair of leather chairs. "Will you have a seat, Mr. Mitcham?"

And then, more light-footed than Mitcham would have expected a man of Thane's size would be, he stepped quickly to the door.

"Mr. Chan!" he called toward the kitchen.

Mitcham couldn't see the front hall from where Thane had just seated him, but he heard a low, curious murmur of voices, then Thane clearing his throat. "Call in the others, please," he said loudly.

Just as clearly, the Chinaman replied in a singsong voice, "Yessir, Missah Thane, right now, right away, Chan call now."

Alone in the parlor, Mitcham got that funny itching on the back of his neck and furrowed his brow. Something wasn't on the level.

He didn't know what it was yet, but he'd figure it out.

Josh wasn't sure but that he wasn't supposed to stand up right about now and shout, "Let's go get the son of a bitch!"

But he didn't.

He couldn't.

He was beginning to think he was a coward.

Grover Detroit had turned out to be an old friend of Slocum's. He'd done a lot of rib-poking and eye-rolling and alluding to something that happened in Amarillo, Texas, especially when a lady called Miss Lola came by the table. But eventually, Detroit had told them what was going on so far as he'd been able to determine.

He'd told them everything he'd figured out so far from Al and the paper and that Foley fellow who was hidden behind the newspaper at the other end of the room.

But when they made the connection between Mitcham and Thane, and that Mitcham was most likely out there right at that very minute; when Josh thought he should have stood up and hollered, he hadn't.

Slocum threw him a look that said he was proud that Josh was staying so cool-headed. Josh couldn't look back. He stared at the tabletop, and his hands, which were all but shaking.

How could he have been so bloodthirsty only a few days ago and so lily-livered now?

Time, he supposed. He was thinking now. And he had Slocum along. But mostly, he was thinking that it wouldn't do his brothers much good if he was to go off and get himself killed, too. His father hadn't had any brothers, after all.

If Josh up and died, there would be no one to carry on the family name. His branch of it, anyway. All that would be left of the Iowa Quaids would be his dull-witted cousin up by Cedar Rapids.

That would be some kind of legacy to leave the future, wouldn't it?

But then, they had Mr. Grover Detroit on their side. Or so he hoped.

"What do you think, Grover?" Slocum was asking

Detroit. "Thane gonna start himself up a range war over this sheep thing?"

Detroit shook his head. "That's all I can figure out. Stupid son of a bitch."

"Well," allowed Slocum as he signaled for another beer, "I don't reckon he can pull it off with just one gun. Bound to be others out there. He's waited too long and he's fighting high odds."

Detroit nodded. "Yeah. But don't forget, most of these ranchers around here ain't fightin' men. I'll bet the majority of 'em are even too young to have fought in the war, and the most any of 'em have fired a pistol is for shootin' snakes and barn rats."

Roughly, Slocum rubbed a hand over his cheek. Josh could practically hear the brush of stubble from where he sat.

"You got a point, Grover. What do you say, Josh? You been awful quiet."

Josh gulped, panicking. "Me?" he said, about an octave higher than he intended.

Slocum tucked his chin and arched a brow. "You see anybody else in here named Josh?"

11

Slocum busied himself putting up the horses at the livery, which turned out to be a five-stall pole barn at the south end of Main Street.

He was a tad worried about Josh, whom he had sent back up to the saloon, saying that he'd see to the boy's horse, Stoney. The kid seemed, over the past few days, to have lost his gusto for tracking down Mitcham. Oh, he was still going, certainly, but that eager-for-blood look was gone from his face.

Probably a good thing, when you got right down to it. He'd be cooler for certain. However, Slocum was wondering what the boy would do when push came to shove.

Not that it mattered. They had already come so far and were so close that he figured to go and take out Mitcham—all alone, if he had to. Mitcham was a mad-dog killer, and wanted, dead or alive, in two states and two territories.

Slocum hadn't confided that part—about there being a reward on the end of this deal—to Josh, mainly because he was afraid the kid's righteous indignation might just boil over the top if he found out that the whole damn southwest wanted Mitcham's ass—or Hendricks's ass, or Keeler's ass or the ass of whatever name he was using at the time—in a sling.

Dead, if possible.

Alive, if you insisted.

Slocum figured to save the New Mexico Territory
the cost of a trial and an execution.

He also intended to go back with a voucher and
collect from the Arizona Territory, too. He'd wire the
two states wanting Mitcham and hope for the best.

But even if only Arizona and New Mexico actually
came through with the rewards on their posters, he'd
be almost twenty thousand richer. Seventeen thousand, five hundred, to be exact. He'd figured to split
it with Josh.

But now that Grover was here—wasn't that something, him just showing up like that?—Slocum was
just as willing to split it three ways.

After all, his grudge against Mitcham was wholly
personal. As long as Mitcham ended up out of commission—permanently—that was enough. The reward money was just a pleasant added bonus.

He put down the brush, picked up a metal comb
and began to work the snarls out of Tubac's tail.

"How a nag with such a scrubby ol' bottle brush
of a tail can get it so tangled up is beyond me, old
son," he muttered.

The horse, busy with his oats, simply snorted in
reply.

Well, Slocum hadn't said anything to Grover Detroit yet, either, about that reward. He would tonight,
though. There was no sense in running straight out to

Thane's ranch when they didn't know the odds, even if he was certain that was where Mitcham had hired out his gun. Slocum was more in favor of letting Thane make the first move, and hopefully, showing his hand.

Besides, the horses deserved the break.

And he deserved a little time with that pretty little humdinger over at the saloon. What was her name?

"Lola," he muttered under his breath, although he muttered it with a smile on his lips. "That's it."

Yes, that was the ticket, he thought as he moved from Tubac's tail, now tangle-free, to his mane. Stoney would be next. Slocum figured to take a little time out to watch and to wait, and to have himself a nice quiet evening—or two or three—with the lovely Lola.

Blackfoot, Mitcham and Siler filed slowly out of the house and onto the porch. Blackfoot quietly closed the door behind them as Siler slapped his hat back on his head.

He had noticed that the other two hadn't taken theirs off until that Chinaman yammered at them, but if he was the only one with any goddamn manners, that only said good about his mama, didn't it?

"You raised up in a barn?" he asked Mitcham as he adjusted his Stetson.

Mitcham looked at him like he was looney. "What the hell you babblin' about?" he snapped.

"Nothin'," said Siler with a shake of his head. "Never mind."

Blackfoot stood there, staring out over the broad, dry valley and the grazing cattle dotting it. He said, "So we start tomorrow."

Siler rolled his eyes. They'd all been standing right there when Thane said it, hadn't they?

"You been out to this O'Brien's place?" Mitcham asked. He asked Blackfoot the question, and pointedly ignored Siler.

"No," Blackfoot replied.

Even though nobody had asked him, Siler volunteered, "I ain't either. Hell, he didn't tell us nothing till just now. Didn't know I was hirin' on to start up a range war." And then he quickly added, "Not that it makes no difference to me. Just as long as I get paid."

Mitcham nodded, and Siler instantly felt like a schoolkid who had just gotten a good score on some test or other.

Now, why the hell did Mitcham make him feel like that?

"I'll go tonight," Blackfoot stated. Not that he ever did anything but state things, the stoic redskin son of a bitch.

"Fine by me," Mitcham said, and walked away, down the porch.

Blackfoot seemed to think this was the end of the conversation, too, because he sat down and picked up his whittling again, which left Siler standing there all by his lonesome, looking like a horse's ass.

"Well, shit!" he muttered, and followed Mitcham down the porch.

Siler was beginning to feel a little riled about the treatment he was getting around here. He was perfectly willing to respect any man who'd proved himself with a gun. But he expected the same in return.

Mitcham and Blackfoot didn't appear to respect anybody but themselves.

Siler sat back down at the chair beside the table, and watched Mitcham's horse's backside, its tail swishing lazily, as Mitcham led it away, to the barn. Well, at least they were finally going to do something, he mused. Get the show on the road. He was all for it, by God.

A range war. It was kind of exciting to be on the instigating side, to be in on it right at the beginning. Hell, he hadn't been in this position for a good long time. Usually, somebody called him in after the parties in question had started kicking up dust and a few bodies had already fallen.

Old Thane had himself a good cause, he supposed. Keeping the range open for cattle was a general good idea, wasn't it? Everybody hated sheep, didn't they?

"What the hell does it matter, anyhow?" he said aloud, to no one but himself.

Slowly, thoughtfully, he picked up the cards and shuffled them. "Just as long as Thane pays," he muttered as he began to deal. "That's all I care about. Period."

Deuce of hearts.
Jack of diamonds.
Three of hearts.

At dusk, Marcus O'Brien waved good night to Julio and made his way up to the house. O'Brien still liked to walk with a shepherd's crook, although it had been some years since he'd actively had need for one, except perhaps at shearing time. He just liked the feel of it in his hand, and the feel as it struck the earth, gaining purchase. It felt solid, right.

He was nearly to the house when RJ, the red merle shepherd dog that tagged at his heels, stopped and looked toward the darkening distant hills. The dog's tail stopped its nearly perpetual wag, and he growled softly, his hackles rising.

O'Brien stopped and stared off in the direction in which the dog was looking.

He saw nothing. It was probably just some vermin. These dogs of his would use any excuse for a frolic, but he was well aware that coyotes were capable of luring a lone dog out beyond the reach of the other dogs or a shepherd, then ambushing it.

RJ was eight years old, and he knew better than to be coaxed into playing that game.

O'Brien bent slightly and ruffled the dog's coat. "Settle down, old fellow," he said. "The flocks are safe. Don't go falling for those old coyote tricks."

O'Brien climbed the porch steps, and after a moment the dog stopped his distance gazing and growling, and followed him up and into the house, from which the smells of roasted lamb and potatoes emanated.

O'Brien poked his head into the kitchen and took a long whiff. "Smells wonderful, lass."

Mrs. Donovan, who was large and broad of beam and hardly a lass at forty-nine, momentarily lost her mind and giggled. She recovered immediately though, O'Brien noticed, and upended her smile into a frown.

"It's about time you showed up," she said, trying to appear put out. "My roast is close to ruined."

As the dog crossed the floor and curled up beside the potbellied stove, O'Brien, trying not to grin, said, "Now, now, Mrs. Donovan. You tell me that each time. And the roast is always perfect. Is there jelly?"

"Of course, there's jelly," she snapped halfheartedly. "I brought you some fresh. And if the roast is always perfect, that's not from your helping it any. There's carrots and peas on the back burner. Potatoes are in with the lamb. And the jelly pot's already on the table."

She untied her apron and took it off, carefully walked around the dog and hung it on a hook behind the stove. "Don't know how you can stand that filthy beast in the house, Marcus O'Brien."

The dog looked up, wiggling his tailless rump at her words.

You understand her, too, old lad, O'Brien thought, smiling. *Not even the mysteries of the female sex can fool a dog.*

"Made you three loaves of bread," Mrs. Donovan said, pointing and three dishcloth-covered loaves. "That should last through Wednesday," she went on. "Reckon you can eat sandwiches out of this till then." She gathered her bag and her shawl.

"And what have you got planned for Wednesday?" O'Brien asked.

"Beef stew," she said. "Mayhap roast beef. Davie'll be butcherin' a steer tomorrow or the next day."

Mrs. Donovan was wife to Davie Donovan, who was O'Brien's nearest neighbor and one of the ranchers who now also ran sheep on his property and the open range. She came over twice a week to see that O'Brien had a hot meal at least that often, and she sometimes brought beef with her.

This was fine with O'Brien, who enjoyed the taste of a good, well-done beef roast now and then.

Of course, it would never replace lamb or mutton, but it was a nice change.

Every once in a while, she fried up a chicken for him, too: an old hen or a young rooster. He mostly kept chickens for the eggs, of which he enjoyed three each morning—freshly hard-boiled and mashed up with butter and salt—along with toast made from her good bread, slathered with mesquite honey or strawberry preserves, when he had them.

He was a creature of habit, was Marcus O'Brien, and he wasn't too much in favor of letting women into his house.

Still, he didn't know what he'd do without Mrs. Donovan.

He walked her out to the front stoop, where Julio was just bringing up her buggy, hitched and ready. RJ followed them out, of course. When the dog wasn't working sheep, he was O'Brien's shadow.

O'Brien helped Mrs. Donovan into her buggy, the smells of his impending dinner tickling at his nose. His stomach was growling, and he was almost ashamed to admit that he was anxious for Mrs. Donovan to be on her way so that he could get down to the business of filling his belly. And have everything back to normal again.

As she gathered her reins, he noticed that RJ was no longer by his side. Instead, the dog was at the far end of the porch, staring off in to the distant hills again, and he was growling.

O'Brien furrowed his brow. Even Mrs. Donovan noticed the dog's behavior.

"What is it, Mr. O'Brien?" she asked. "Coyotes?"

"Likely," O'Brien said. But why would a coyote still be in the same place? A healthy animal would have jogged out of smell and sight range—even for the sharp-nosed, eagle-eyed dog—long ago. Perhaps it was sick.

That was all he needed. A rabid coyote wandering around.

"Julio?"

The lean Mexican man at the buggy's head looked away from the hills and said, *"Sí?"*

"Mayhap we should check on that," O'Brien said. "Might be a sick coyote. He was up there, in right about the same place, earlier. Why don't you take one of the other fellows and—"

Julio waved a hand. "Everyone is out with the flocks except for myself and old Juanito. And he is elbow deep into making the frijoles and enchiladas. I will go up and check."

"I'll go with you, then," said O'Brien.

Mrs. Donovan's head fairly snapped toward him. "You will not, Marcus O'Brien. You'll march into that house right now and eat your supper. I will not have my lovely lamb roast turned into a cinder over some lurking, sickly vermin. It doesn't take two men to put one slug into a coyote."

"Yes, ma'am," both Julio and O'Brien said at once. Mrs. Donovan could be a commanding presence when she wanted to be. There were times when O'Brien got a chuckle out of her—and he always got a good meal out of her visits—but most often, he swore he didn't understand why Davie Donovan didn't take an axe to her.

"I go now," Julio said.

RJ made a tentative move to follow him, but O'Brien said, "Down, RJ," and the dog dropped immediately. That was the last thing he needed, his RJ getting bit by some rabid animal.

Mrs. Donovan, despite her objections to having him in the house, felt much the same way, because she said, "Good boy."

It was her husband, Davie, who had shot RJ's sire those many years ago, and who had later apologized so profusely. O'Brien had long ago forgiven Davie, but it seemed that the Donovans were still in a state of regret over the matter.

Julio wandered off toward the barn to collect his horse and his rifle and, O'Brien supposed, tell old Juanito to take his time with getting the supper ready.

"Good evening, then," said Mrs. Donovan.

"Good night, and thank you," O'Brien replied. "Drive safely, Mrs. Donovan."

"Always do," she grumbled as she slapped her dapple-gray horse's rump with the reins. "Get up, Belle. I'll see you come Wednesday, Mr. O'Brien," she called as she drove off.

O'Brien stayed out on the porch until she was out of sight, and Julio had emerged from the barn and set off toward the hills. Only then did he go into the house, taking RJ with him, and settle down to his lamb.

Of which RJ got a goodly share.

12

When Slocum walked back up to the saloon, Josh was nowhere in sight. Grover Detroit was, though.

Slocum joined him at his table.

"Where's Junior?" Slocum asked as he signaled the barkeep for a beer. He scanned the room quickly, looking for Lola, but didn't see her, either. Suddenly annoyed, he said, "He ain't upstairs with that little gal, is he?"

Detroit snorted. "Hell, no," he said. "Don't know where the hell she disappeared to, but Josh's down the street at the Cornerstone Café, which I gather is the only place, decent or otherwise, to get a hot meal in this fair city. Said he was starvin' to death, and couldn't wait any longer. Hell, you took so long, he's probably on his way back up here."

Detroit leaned back in his chair. "I kinda thought it was on the rude side, myself, seein' as how you were tendin' his mount and all."

Al brought the beer, and Slocum took a sip. "Don't matter," he said, scowling into his glass. No matter how much you drank of it, it never got any better. "After I finish up this, I believe I'll go down and join him. You ate yet?"

"Just waitin' for you," Detroit said with a grin.

"Unlike a few other people I could mention, I got manners."

"Grover?" Slocum asked after he took a long drink, then wiped his mouth on the back of his sleeve.

"That's my name."

"You reckon they got a sheriff in this town?"

Detroit grinned. "Wondered when somebody was gonna get round to askin' that. Al, here, says the jail's up the street about a half block."

Slocum nodded, then hesitated. "Say, there's no paper out on you in New Mexico, is there?"

Detroit shook his head, his smile never wavering. "Not that I know of. How 'bout you?"

"You're funny as a crutch, Grover," Slocum said dryly. He polished off his beer and stood up, the chair scraping noisily in the nearly empty barroom.

Detroit stood, too. He said, "So, which one first? The sheriff or supper?"

Slocum sighed. His belly had been grumbling for a half hour. "Aw, hell," he said. "I'm too hungry to be law-abidin' right at the moment. Let's see if we can't catch up with Josh."

"I'm right behind you, buddy," Detroit said, and snatching up his neatly folded newspaper, he followed Slocum out the batwing doors.

But Josh wasn't at the Cornerstone Café. The counterman told them that yes, a young man had been in and eaten some supper, then left word that he was all dragged out and was going up to the hotel to turn in.

"Awful goddamn early to be turnin' in," Detroit

commented. He took a look at his pocket watch. "Hell, it's only a quarter to eight!"

Slocum figured the kid was just trying to put a little space between himself and the force of vengeance, and he said, "Reckon he just needs time to think things over."

He picked a table by the window—not that anyone was at any of the others, for they were the only customers in the place—and sat down. Detroit pulled out the chair opposite.

"What you gents wantin' tonight?" the counterman asked. "We got good biscuits and gravy."

Detroit appeared to be studying the chalkboard menu, but Slocum asked, "What you got in the way of beef? That's edible, I mean."

"Steaks," replied the counterman. He slapped his dishtowel over his shoulder, then leaned on the counter. "Steaks is always good. Got a decent beef stew, too."

Slocum ordered a steak with all the trimmings, and Detroit ordered the stew, and before Detroit could start needling him about Josh again, Slocum changed the subject in a way he knew would get Detroit's attention.

"There's a good-sized reward on Mitcham, you know," he said as he pulled out his fixings pouch. He proceeded to roll himself a quirlie.

Detroit's brow went up. "In New Mexico?" he asked. "I knew there was money on him over in Arizona."

Slocum nodded. "Texas and Kansas, too. Guess he musta missed out on shootin' somebody in the Indian Territory."

Grover Detroit's mouth crooked up into a smile. "Sloppy of him."

Slocum gave a lick to his quirlie, then stuck it between his lips and struck a match. He puffed the smoke into life. "You gonna ask me how much," he said, shaking out the lucifer, "or did you all of a sudden go philanthropic on me?"

Detroit's grin broadened. "Reckon I'll bite. How much?"

An hour later, stomachs filled with better-than-average grub, they walked back up to the jail. Slocum took a peek inside the bar along the way, and was glad to see Lola sitting down at the end of it. She looked dejected, but Slocum figured she'd light up if somebody were to sling some business her way.

Which he planned to, as soon as he got this out of the way.

When they entered the sheriff's office, the man dozing behind the desk, his chair cocked back on two legs, his arms folded over his chest, woke just enough to open one eye and grunt at them. He was an odd sort, wearing a worn out stovepipe hat—instead of the usual Stetson—a spade beard and a bright red shirt, neatly ironed.

"You the law around here?" Detroit asked.

"I am," said the man, opening his other eye. They

were icy gray, Slocum noticed. Looked to be cold as tombstones, too.

"Then we've got business with you," Slocum said. He walked forward, to the other side of the desk, and stuck out his hand. "Name's Slocum. This here is Detroit."

The fellow behind the desk didn't take his hand, however, although he angled forward some. The front legs of his chair hit the floor with a bang. "I'm Sheriff Davis. State your case."

Marcus O'Brien had nearly fallen asleep in his rocking chair when somebody started rattling the door with his knuckles.

Groggily, O'Brien rose and, swearing under his breath, crossed the room. It was probably Julio, although why he should chose this particular time to report in—when O'Brien had heard the report of his gun practically an hour ago—was a puzzle. Why did a man need to report a dead coyote, anyway?

But those knuckles kept rapping on the door, and he opened it.

He was surprised to find old Juanito standing on his porch, floppy hat turning nervously in his walnut-colored hands. "*Patron?*" he said, before O'Brien had a chance to open his mouth.

"What is it, Juanito?" O'Brien asked. He had a feeling it couldn't be good. Juanito was shy, and had only come up to the house on two other occasions during his employment of seven years' standing: once to report he'd stumbled over six dead ewes, and once to let O'Brien know that another of the shepherds had broken a leg.

Juanito being on the porch, especially at this time of night, couldn't be a good thing.

And it wasn't. "It is Julio," the old Mexican shepherd said. "He has not yet returned. He said he would only be a half hour to get that coyote. I hear the shot, but he does not come."

O'Brien was wide awake by this time. He nodded curtly, then said, "Come in, Juanito, while I fetch us some lanterns."

Sheriff Davis, who had appeared to be mentally going over his wanted posters all the time Slocum was explaining the situation, softened just a bit.

"All right," he said. "I admit it sounds suspicious, but you know as well as I that I can't go gallivanting out to Thane's place and hauling off these supposed gunmen just on your word."

Slocum hadn't really expected the local law to do anything, but still, he was annoyed. Actually, he'd been annoyed since Davis had ignored his offer of a handshake. And now it seemed that Davis was a coward as well.

Detroit, on Slocum's right, piped up, "Well, now, Sheriff Davis, seein' as there's paper out on this Mitcham character, and seein' as he's wanted dead or alive, it seems to me that you got every right in the world to ride on out there anytime you want."

Davis arched a brow, and his stovepipe tilted precariously. "Just go out there and plug him, I suppose."

Detroit grinned. "That's about the size of it."

Davis frowned and Slocum said, "Dammit, Grover, stop helpin'."

"Be a good idea if you listened to your friend, Mr. Detroit," Davis said. "This fella Mitcham hasn't done anything illegal in my town." His fingers tapped the desktop. "Yet, anyway. If he does, that might be another matter. But I ain't gonna court trouble. This is a quiet town. Want to keep it that way."

Seeing as how they had just alerted the man to a possible range war brewing, Slocum figured that Davis was only going to get his way for maybe the next twenty-four hours.

And Sheriff Davis hadn't been able to tell them anything they hadn't already learned about the elusive Mr. Thane. The man was a regular mystery, even to the two men who should know just about everybody in town—the local barman and the sheriff.

Slocum stood up from the window ledge he'd been leaning against. "All right, Sheriff," he said, cutting off the meeting before Detroit said something else wise and got them both arrested. "But we just thought you oughta be warned. Trouble's brewin'."

Detroit stood up, too.

The sheriff didn't move out of his chair. To Slocum, he said, "Well, you told me. I don't know Thane more than to nod at him twice a year, but seems to me he'd be shootin' himself in the foot if he was to start trouble out there. Cattle and sheep get along fine out here, Slocum. I think Thane's convinced of that."

Detroit opened up his mouth, but Slocum was close enough, right then, to step on his toe.

"Youch!" bellowed Detroit as Slocum shoved him out the door.

"You need us, we'll be at the hotel," Slocum said to Davis, and closed the door between them. "Dammit, Grover!"

"Seems to me that I'm the one who ought to be damnin' you for busting my toes altogether," Detroit replied through gritted teeth. On the boardwalk, he stood on one foot. The other was upturned and cradled in his hand.

"Aw, Christ," Slocum said with a shake of his head. "When you gonna learn to keep your trap closed, Grover? That sheriff is no help whatsoever, but he'd sure be a hindrance if he was to lock us up."

Slocum started down the walk, toward Lola and the saloon, and Detroit, hopping on one foot, tried to keep up with him.

"What the hell's he gonna lock us up *for*?" Detroit asked, frowning.

"I just had a feeling that if we stuck around long enough, arguin' with him, he'd figure out some reason. I didn't like the way he kept peerin' over toward the poster board."

"We're not wanted here," Detroit said peevishly.

They stopped, having reached the saloon. Slocum put his hand on the door and quickly looked inside.

Lola was still there, and still unoccupied. Good.

He said, "Grover, go on up to the hotel or come in and have a drink. I don't care. But just don't pester me about this dumb-cluck sheriff until tomorrow, all right? I done enough of my civic duty for one day."

He went through the doors and walked straight up to Lola, who grinned at him.

He sat down next to her, then cocked his hat back with his thumb. "Evenin', Miss Lola," he said, grinning right back at her. "Might I have the pleasure of buyin' you a drink?"

Marcus O'Brien and old Juanito were on foot, lanterns held high, as they finally crossed the valley looking for the lost Julio. They followed RJ, who seemed to know where he was going, even if they didn't. Repeatedly, the dog ran out ahead, far from their ring of lantern light, only to double back and come within ten feet of them, barking sharply and loudly, as if to scold them for not being faster.

What had started out as a bad feeling had, for O'Brien, worsened with every step. Now it was all he could do to pick up one foot and put it in front of the other.

Fear had nothing to do with it, unless you counted the fear of what he half-expected to find. But fear, physical fear for himself? Of this, Marcus O'Brien had not one whit. He had brought sheep into cattle country, after all. That wasn't a job for cowards.

It might be a job for fools, though, he thought as

Julio's horse suddenly appeared in the ring of light from their upraised lanterns. Riderless, the horse ambled up to them.

O'Brien and Juanito exchanged uneasy glances.

O'Brien went to the horse and took its reins. The rifle was still in the boot. He pulled it down and checked it: It hadn't been fired.

Right at that moment, a feeling like ice water went through him. He stood for a moment, listening to the dog bark at them frantically. He rested his forehead on the saddle seat, and then he turned toward Juanito.

"You wait here," he said. "I'm going . . ." But he stopped, because Juanito was pointing straight at him, his finger outstretched and trembling.

"*Patrón?*" the old man said in a breaking voice. He quickly crossed himself. "Blood. On your face."

O'Brien touched his forehead, and his fingers came away red. He lifted the lantern high then, and held it over the saddle. It was peppered with fat drops and runners of blood.

"Dear God," breathed O'Brien.

To the sound of RJ's furious barking, O'Brien cleaned the saddle as best he could with his sleeve, then hoisted himself up into it. He didn't often ride, so it was something of a struggle, but at last he looked down at Juanito. "Wait here, old friend," he said.

Nudging the horse with his heels, he grimly followed the dog up into the gentle hills.

13

Lola, when all was said and done, was one mighty fine piece of work.

Of course, he hadn't said or done it all, not by a long shot. Hell, he'd hardly even started! But he was pretty sure he was safe in making that prediction about her.

As she led him up the steep stairs, her backside swishing in his face invitingly, he reluctantly turned his head back down the stairs to toward the door. He half-expected to see Grover outside, leaning against a post, but the sidewalk was empty.

"C'mon, cowboy," Lola cooed, and he forgot all about Grover Detroit. He gained a dark, narrow landing and followed Lola down an equally dark hallway.

The whole place, in fact, seemed to be falling apart, and he wondered, momentarily, if the festivities he had planned might not literally bring the house down.

However, there wasn't time to dwell on it, because just then, Lola opened a door and ushered him into her room.

"Nice," he said in surprise.

The lamps inside were lit, bathing the rose-colored bed and curtain and chair in a soft, golden glow. She had a four-poster up here, although how they'd gotten it up the stairs was beyond him. There was a broad, marble-topped dresser with a wide mirror that was just starting to flake its silver, and a matching chifforobe.

The room was neat and tidy, and had a green, tasseled chair as well as the rose one, and a little writing desk near the window.

The only out-of-place thing was a precarious stack of papers and books and such, nearly a foot tall and perched on the edge of the desk.

Slocum took off his hat, a gesture Lola seemed to appreciate. She took his hat from him and hung it on a peg by the door. She said, "Thanks. I like to keep it homey. Now, what did you have in mind?"

He smiled at her. "The night. How much?"

Lola's dark eyes widened and her brows flew up. "The whole night?"

Slocum supposed that in a town this size, she must not get much business. And when she did, it was most likely a ranch hand in a hurry.

"The whole night," he said. "I want to sleep in a soft bed with a soft, willin' body in it."

He almost added, *and I'd like to get started on that about an hour ago.* He held his tongue, however.

Lola's finger went to her chin and her eyes lidded for a moment. Then she looked up at him. "Would twenty dollars be too much? I haven't ever had an overnighter before."

"Twenty would be fine," Slocum said, and took her into his arms.

She was soft and she was sweet, and he liked the fact that she still had some shyness left in her. A surprising amount, in fact, for somebody plying her trade. She made him turn his back while she got into bed, and then blow out the last of the candles before he joined her.

Even though he hadn't exactly seen her naked as yet, she sure felt good when he joined her. Slocum's hands prowled over full, round, breasts set high and proud, and caressed nipples tight with desire. While he settled in to lap and nuzzle at her breast, his hands discovered a tiny waist, then a soft bell of lean hips and surprisingly taut thighs.

She gasped a little when his fingers slipped between her legs, then again when he gently parted her and inserted a tentative finger. It was met with a slippery gush of wet and warmth, and an encouraging movement of her hips.

He took her mouth again, kissing her firmly, hungrily, tongue against searching tongue, and slipped his knees between hers.

"Yesssss," she hissed when he entered her smoothly and surely. She was tight, but it was a good tight. She held him as firmly as a greased handshake, and he began to move.

She moved with him, catching his rhythm and bending to it, rising to meet him, tilting and angling her pelvis to make the most of his every thrust. Her sweat-slippery legs slid against his hips and his thighs as she began to lose herself in the coupling, and she craned her head back, opened her mouth.

He thrust deeply now, burying himself to the root in her warmth, and felt the itch in his loins building, building toward a fiery conflagration.

And just when he was about to explode, she suddenly arched her back and clenched her inner muscles spasmodically, and in her climax carried him over the edge.

They lay still for a few moments, Slocum still inside her, and the only sound was that of their animal panting. He could still feel her internal spasms gripping then releasing him over and over.

It had taken Slocum by surprise, but he was in favor of surprises when they were good ones. And this one surely had been. And would continue to be, if he had anything to say about it.

Softly, she whispered into his ear, "T-thank you."

He turned his face toward hers. "No, honey. Thank *you*."

"You don't understand," she said quietly. "See, I never . . . That is, I've never in my life . . . What I mean to say is that before, only the men had a . . . a good time. I didn't know it could be like that."

He couldn't be sure, but he was pretty sure that she blushed in the darkness.

"So, thank you," she finished.

Now Slocum was puzzled. He rolled off her and put his arm around her shoulders, drawing her near. He arranged the covers about them while he thought.

Well, it would explain her modesty, he supposed.

"Just how long you been plying this trade, Lola?" he asked.

"Four months," she said in a small voice. "I'm sorry. Does it show?"

He gave her shoulders a squeeze. "Darlin', it was great. And, I reckon it'll be great again, once I build up another head of steam."

She shifted her head to look at him. "Again?"

She didn't look in the least disturbed, though.

Grinning, Slocum said, "Just how come you got into this business, anyhow?"

She shrugged. "I used to be the schoolteacher up at Hanging Rock. I'd been out here for less than three months when a half dozen cowboys, liquored up, came into town shooting their pistols into the air, looking for a good time. I guess they thought a young, untouched schoolmarm was it."

She had turned her head away, and Slocum reached to cup her chin and turn her face gently back toward him. At last, her eyes met his.

"I'm sorry," she said. "I don't mean to burden you with my troubles. I never told a . . . a customer before."

"That's all right, sweetie," he said, genuinely touched and concerned. "I'm sorry for your troubles. All men ain't like those cowhands who . . . who mussed you up."

"I know," she replied. "I know. The women were almost worse, when they found out."

Slocum tried to think of something soothing to say,

but he drew a blank. So he just lay there a good long while and held her.

O'Brien sat on one side of the body, which they had brought down to the house and laid out on the dining room table. Juanito stood on the opposite side, his hat in his hands. They both said nothing for a very long time.

And then, in hardly more than a mumble, Juanito said, "I should go to the town now?"

O'Brien shook his head. "No. I'll go in the morning. Not that it will do any good. You know how Sheriff Davis feels about . . ."

"I know," replied Juanito. His eyes were cast down, but his voice was filled with quiet venom. "I know how he feels about my kind."

O'Brien leaned forward to rest his elbow on his knees. "Davis is an idiot, Juanito."

"I know that too, *Patrón*."

Again, they lapsed into silence. At last, O'Brien broke it.

"You can go on down to the bunkhouse, Juanito," he said, rising. "And put Julio's horse up, please."

Juanito hesitated. "I do not like to leave my friend alone, *Señor* O'Brien."

O'Brien moved to Juanito's side. He put a hand on the old shepherd's shoulder, and said softly, "He won't be alone. I'll be with him."

Slowly, Juanito nodded. "I should go and tell the others, then."

O'Brien had been so shocked by the killing—one slug, which had entered Julio's back and emerged from his chest, and most likely ripped his grand and gracious heart apart in its passage—that he hadn't got that far in his thinking.

He said, "Yes, of course. Tell them to be on their guard."

Juanito stepped sluggishly toward the door, his stoop more pronounced than ever. His hand on the latch, he turned back toward O'Brien. "I do not understand. Who could have done this?"

O'Brien could only think of one man, but he held his tongue and instead answered, "It might have been someone wandering through, Juanito."

"But to kill him and not even take his money? There was twenty dollars in his purse. Or take the horse he rode? I do not think so, *Patrón*. You and I both know who it was. Even after all this time, we both know."

"He must have gone mad," O'Brien muttered.

"He has always been mad," Juanito said as he walked out the door, into the night.

Slocum came, good and hard, for the second time that night, and he was once again accompanied by the sad and lovely Lola.

Between their two bouts of lovemaking, she had told him how she had come to be there. The citizens of the place she'd been before, the place she'd been raped, had forced her out.

It was the women of the community, mostly.

It usually was.

She had no money, schoolteaching not being a profession to command much in the way of compensation. She had no family—at least, none that would have her after what had befallen her in Hanging Rock—and no place to go.

So she'd come here and taken up the only profession, other than schoolmarm, available to the majority of women out here.

She was now Cholla's town whore.

But amazingly enough, she seemed to have taken it in stride. She'd been desperately hurt by what was done to her—the aftermath more than the actual rape, Slocum thought—but she'd faced up to it, decided what to do, and she'd done it. She did it with no apologies to anyone, and with no shame.

He figured that the only reason she'd mentioned it at all was because she was so surprised by the feelings and sensations he'd brought out in her. He hadn't known her long, but he figured he'd known her long enough to ascertain that she was smart, she was good-hearted, and she was a realist.

She was also the best piece of tail for miles around. And she was more eager than ever, after she'd at last felt what she should have been feeling all along.

Slocum rolled off her and reached over to push a stray strand of hair out of her eyes. She was still breathing hard, and purring like a cat full of cream.

"Slocum," she panted happily, "you are a man of many miracles."

"Thank you, ma'am," he replied, grinning. "Just might have another one in me. 'Specially if you'd allow me to turn on a light and have a smoke."

Surprisingly, the girl who had made him turn his back while she undressed and who had made him blow out all the lamps before he joined her, struck a match and lit the lamp beside the bed. And she didn't even bother to pull up her covers before she did it.

"Do you like cigars?" she asked.

Struck dumb, he nodded.

She was even more beautiful than she had felt. The bed linen slung carelessly over her hip, she rolled a little to the side to open a drawer in her bedside table and pluck a cigar from it. Her body was lean and lightly muscled, yet deliciously curvaceous in all the right places. Right now, it glistened gold with a thin skin of sweat in the lamplight.

She turned toward him and offered the cigar, which he took. "Lola, honey," he said, "you are some kind of woman."

Her brows went up, as if that comment had taken her by surprise and tickled her a little, too. As he bit off the cigar's end, she struck another sulphurtip.

"Thanks," she said. She held the match while he lit his cigar. "But there's some argument about what kind of woman I am."

"Not with me, there ain't," Slocum replied. "You're the finest kind, Lola. The finest kind."

14

All alone, Josh Quaid lay in his darkened hotel room, thinking.

He was thinking about back home, in Iowa, and what it would be like there, this time of year. He was wondering how his small hard of cattle—both dairy and beef—were doing, and if his uncle had slaughtered yet.

He was wondering, too, about Allison Grant, that pretty little neighbor girl his brothers had teased him about for the last couple of years, ever since she'd moved to Iowa. Had she gone ahead and married Homer Woolridge, like she always threatened to?

Josh had a feeling it was mostly bluff, but you never could tell with women. He'd written her once from Omaha, but he hadn't stuck around long enough to get a reply. That was when he and he brothers were just starting out to sow their wild oats, when everything was still new and fun and sort of glamorous.

When he still had brothers.

When he still had a mother and a father who were alive.

Silently, a tear slipped down his cheek, and he rubbed it away coarsely. He was a grown man now, the only Quaid of his branch left alive. Quaids didn't cry like babies.

He hadn't cried, had he? Not when they heard about Ma and Pa, not when he woke in the doc's office and Doc told him about Earl and Joe being gone.

No, sir. He'd kept a stiff upper lip.

Another tear skittered down his cheek, but he barely noticed.

It was hitting him at once. There was nobody left. Nobody but him.

A quiet sob escaped him, and suddenly, he rolled over on his cot and wept, without shame, into his pillow.

Grover Detroit wasn't sleeping, either. He was out in front of the hotel on a wooden chair, which he had cocked back and was balancing on two legs while he smoked his pipe.

He stared off into the distance, across the street, but he wasn't focused on the shop signs or the storefronts. He had one of those itchy feelings again, like something was about to happen. Or had happened.

And it wasn't good.

That Sheriff Davis hadn't done much to alleviate his itch, either. The dumb bastard. Detroit had seen his kind before, and he imagined Slocum had, too. Davis didn't want anybody to upset his applecart, didn't want anybody to make him do any actual work. He was content to let things roll along, and if something like a range war should really happen to take place? Hell, he'd probably take advantage of the situation by taking himself on an extended vacation.

Detroit supposed the whole thing would be left up to the three of them. Well, the two of them. You couldn't count that kid altogether. He was looking a little green around the edges and a little yellow down the spine.

Of course, Detroit couldn't really blame him. Slocum had told him the whole story over dinner, about the kid's folks dying, and then his brothers being murdered by this self-same Mitcham.

Detroit shook his head, although there was no one to see. That would throw a wrench into any kid's system.

Still, he figured that Slocum and he were probably capable of handling the situation by themselves, if push came to shove. Especially now that Slocum had told him about the rewards. Seventeen-five, just for the Territories! That was something to crow about, wasn't it?

And what Slocum hadn't said—but what they'd both been thinking, if he knew Slocum—was that if Mitcham was out there, he wasn't alone. And those other guns were bound to have a reward on them, too.

He could practically see blissful retirement just peeking over the horizon, and giving him a jaunty wave of encouragement.

He was getting too old for this trade. Too old for those Johnny-come-lately shootists who seemed to pop up in every other town he went through. And he was getting slower. He knew it, even if nobody else did.

He had the first stirrings of arthritis in his hands. It didn't bother him all the time, but sometimes it kicked up a real fuss with his knuckles. Felt like a bunch of goddamn pokers sticking in them. He didn't know how many years he had left before he wouldn't be able to draw a gun, much less fire one.

And so it had been pretty near music to his old ears to hear about that reward. He'd like to retire down to Mexico, that's what. It was warm there most all the time, the señoritas were pretty, the mescal was good, and a dollar stretched past forever. Grover Detroit figured he could live like a king for a good long time on a third of seventeen thousand, five hundred dollars.

Plus whatever the states kicked in. Plus whatever those other vermin out there were worth.

His pipe had gone out, and he knocked it against the chair's arm, then stuck it in his pocket. He let his chair drop to all fours with a bang, then stood up. He threw his arms wide and yawned, then quietly entered the hotel, walked past the dozing room clerk and went upstairs to his room.

Latham Siler and Jack Mitcham were waiting out on the porch of Thane's ranch house when Blackfoot rode up. In fact, he was practically sitting in their laps before they realized he was there.

"Well?" asked Mitcham.

Right to the goddamn point, Siler thought. *Don't nobody ever say hello no more?*

"Howdy, Blackfoot," he muttered, after the fact. Better late than never, he figured.

Blackfoot studied them. "After I put the horse away," he said at last, then reined away from them and jogged toward the barn.

Siler shrugged. "Musta been a big nothin'," he said.

"Nope," said Mitcham. This time, instead of wandering back down to his perch at the opposite end of the porch, he pulled out one of Siler's chairs and sat down at the table. Siler was beginning to think of them as his chairs now, anyhow.

"If it had been nothin'," Mitcham continued, "he woulda just rode to the bunkhouse and gone to sleep."

"And left us sittin' here?" Siler asked.

"Yup."

Siler didn't say anything about Blackfoot being one rude son of a bitch, but he would have liked to. At this point, he figured it wasn't any too smart to press his luck. Not with these two yahoos, anyway. He had the distinct feeling they'd just as soon shoot him as say hello.

What the hell ever happened to honor among thieves, anyhow?

Well, maybe he wasn't a thief, and maybe they weren't either, but there ought to be some saying about honor among outlaws. Or at least some kind of politeness.

They waited in silence then, Siler not wanting to

rile Mitcham. And Mitcham, well, just not talking. That was, until Blackfoot wandered back up and pulled out a third chair.

Siler was torn between irritation that they'd invaded his space, and pride.

Mostly, he felt stupid.

But he listened anyhow.

"Watched the house," Blackfoot began. "Big house, only one man in it. He has a woman that comes in to cook or clean, maybe both. Don't know how often."

"What about hands?" Siler asked, suddenly eager for the game to start.

Mitcham threw him an irritated glance, but Blackfoot said, "Only two. Now one. The rest were out with the sheep."

This time, Mitcham beat Siler to it. "What d'you mean, now one?"

"Shot him." Blackfoot leaned back. "Any coffee?"

"No," said Siler. "Everybody's gone to bed."

"What d'you mean, you shot him?" Mitcham insisted.

"I was hid out. One of those damn dogs of his sensed me."

"Whose dog?" Siler asked.

"O'Brien's," Blackfoot snapped.

"Just askin'," said Siler apologetically.

"Mexican came riding up the hill to find out what was bothering the dog. I shot him." Suddenly, Blackfoot swept an arm out over the table, brushing to the side all of Siler's playing cards. He picked up Siler's long-empty glass and placed in on the edge of the table. "This is where we are," he said.

His pocketknife came out, and he put it at the center of the table. "This is O'Brien's place."

"How far?" Mitcham asked.

"Maybe four, four and a half miles," Blackfoot replied. "Shorter by road than the way I went."

He proceeded to lay out landmarks, sometimes using Siler's cards, sometimes using objects from his pockets, and talking, in a terse, broken fashion, about how they would start in the morning.

In silence, Siler watched along with the slightly more verbal Mitcham, but he kept thinking one thought: *It's already started.*

None of them could have noticed the open upstairs window, or the hand that drew back the curtain. And the nodding head that accompanied the hand. They could not see Kim Chan, Thane's humble servant, from their vantage point. Neither could he see them. But he could certainly see them—and hear their voices.

And as he listened, he smiled.

A door creaked behind him, and he turned to see a sleep-rumpled Thane exiting his room and poking a tentative head into the hallway.

"What is it?" Thane asked, rubbing his eyes. "What's going on?"

"Nothing," Chan whispered, lest the men down on

the porch hear him. His English was perfect. "Go back to bed."

"Yes, sir," said Thane, and backing up, he closed the door behind him.

"That's better," muttered Chan, and went back to eavesdropping.

15

Early the next morning and all alone, Marcus O'Brien rode into town. It was seven-thirty when he tied his horse to the hitching post in front of the town jail, and seven-thirty-five before Davis's young deputy, Bill Clancy, unlocked the door.

All muddleheaded and sleepy, his dark hair sticking up every which way, Bill yawned his way around a "Howdy, Marcus," before he swung the door wide. "C'mon in. What bring you to town so early in the mornin'? Hang on, and I'll brew us up a pot of Arbuckle's," he added.

"No time," said O'Brien, although Clancy was already filling the pot with water.

Grinning sleepily, Clancy scooped in the coffee. "How come? One'a them sheep of yours break the law or somethin'?"

"No," O'Brien said. "One of my hands was murdered last night."

Clancy dropped the coffeepot on the stove lid hard enough to make it ring. "What did you say?"

"Last night, my RJ dog was growling at a spot out opposite the house. Figured it was a coyote. Then later, when I stepped outside again to see Mrs. Donovan on her way, the dog was still growling. At the

same place. So then I figured it was a sick coyote,"
O'Brien went on. "Not moving, and all. So I sent
Julio across and up the hill to see to it."

Clancy was all ears now.

"I heard a shot not long after, and I figured Julio
had taken care of the problem and gone back down
to the bunkhouse. Juanito was making his supper."

"That Juanito, he's a pretty good cook," interjected
Clancy. "I ain't never had such good enchiladas in all
my borned days. And I've eaten me a heap of enchiladas."

"Yeah," O'Brien went on. "Except that after a
while, Juanito came up to the house, looking for Julio.
He hadn't turned up."

Clancy's face darkened, and O'Brien continued, "I
found him. One shot in the back. Went right through
his heart and came out his chest. Died instant, I suppose. Least, I hope so."

Clancy sat silently for a moment, arms crossed,
eyes on the floor, before he looked up and asked,
"You got any idea who done it?"

"I think we've both got a fairly good idea, Bill,"
O'Brien said quietly.

"Yup. Reckon we do. But like Sheriff Davis says,
a court needs proof. 'Sides, for the life of me, I can't
imagine ol' Vance Thane lyin' on his belly on the
weeds, gettin' his fancy suit all mussed up, and waitin' for somebody to come lookin' for him so's he
could plug him. Hell, I can't even imagine him lyin'

on his belly! The pressure of it would likely suffocate the fat son of a bitch."

O'Brien scratched his head. "Got a point there, Bill. Well, maybe he's hired some new help. Anybody new in town? Or pass through?"

Clancy scrunched up his face, as if trying to remember something. It seemed that he did, because he said, "Sheriff Davis said as how there was a couple of strangers in here last night, all het up about a man named Mitcham."

And then, quite suddenly, Clancy looked thunderstruck. "Say, they were saying as how they thought somebody was gonna start up a range war, and this Mitcham feller was part of it! You don't suppose that Vance Thane hired Mitcham, do you? He's supposed to be one nasty character, no lie."

O'Brien let out a long sigh through his nose. "And I suppose Davis just brushed them off?"

Clancy shrugged. "Well, you know the sheriff."

"That's what I figured. Where are these gentlemen staying? In town, I hope."

"They said they could be found up at the hotel," Clancy replied. He grabbed his hat and stuck it over his sleep-tousled hair. "You goin' up there?"

"Yes."

"Then I'm goin' with you."

Mitcham checked his rifle for the second time, then stuck it down into its saddle boot. He was filled with something akin to excitement. In the stall across from him, Blackfoot was checking his rifle. In the stall to the right, Siler gave a last tug to his girth strap.

As one, they unlatched their stall doors, and then, one by one, they led their mounts from the barn and out into the morning light. It was still crisp outside, and they all wore jackets.

Mitcham announced, "Let's go kill us some sheep."

He mounted, and the others followed suit. It seemed he was their leader, and he hadn't had to fight anybody for it. Blackfoot and Siler just took orders, which was dandy with him. He wasn't much of a follower.

They set out toward the west, toward the free range land. Thane had specifically warned them against mayhem on private property, although he didn't seem that mad when Blackfoot told him about killing the Mexican. Maybe Thane figured Mexicans didn't count.

Mitcham figured that was all right with him. Killing sheep didn't promise to be much fun—it'd be like shooting fish in a barrel. But what promised to happen after they'd polished off enough of those damned bleating woollies? That would be different.

They rode in silence and in single file: Mitcham in the lead, followed by Blackfoot, with Siler bringing up the rear. After about an hour of this, they came to the big red rocks that Thane had told them marked the end of private land and the beginning of open range.

"All right, boys," Mitcham said, adjusting his hat.

"Let's find some sheep. I don't care whose they are or who's with 'em. Just shoot 'em. And shoot anybody that gets in your way. Got it?"

Blackfoot nodded curtly.

Siler sighed, but he said, "Got it. You want we should split up?"

"Might's well," Mitcham replied.

Siler nodded, and reined his mount off toward the north.

"Back here, 'bout four o'clock!" Mitcham shouted after him.

Siler just nodded and kept on riding away. He kicked his mount into a slow jog. He surely was an odd duck, that Siler. He was either as quiet as death itself, or he was jabbering your ear off. Mostly, about nothing.

Mitcham turned toward Blackfoot.

Blackfoot just grunted at him, then wheeled his horse and galloped south.

His hands crossed over his saddle horn, Mitcham sighed.

"So much for the formalities," he muttered to himself. "Best get on with it."

Giving his horse a dig with his spurs, he cantered off, straight ahead.

"Just hold your horses!" Slocum shouted through the door. Whoever was on the other side was making a god-awful racket. He got his pants on and his gunbelt strapped into place before he threw a look over Lola's way to make sure she was covered up decent. And then he opened the door.

Josh, who was just about to knock again, practically fell in on him.

Slocum caught and righted him, and only then did he notice Detroit and a couple of other men. One of the men looked vaguely familiar, but he couldn't place him right off.

"See you got yourself a few new scars since last time I seen you," Detroit quipped.

Slocum grunted and grabbed for his shirt. "What the hell you boys want?" he asked as he shrugged into it. "Say hello to Miss Lola."

Josh touched his hat and said, "Ma'am." The others just nodded in her direction.

"You fellers mind waitin' in the hall for a second?" he asked, although the tone wasn't that of a question.

Grover Detroit, at least, sensed his irritation, and stepped back, pushing the others with him. Slocum closed the door.

"Sorry, Lola," he said, tucking in his shirt.

She sat up on the bed, hugging the covers to her chin. "It's all right," she said. "Friends of yours?"

"Yeah." He grabbed his hat, then settled it on his head. He dug a hand down into his pocket. "Listen, Lola, I don't want anybody to . . . That is, I want to take up all your time while I'm in town." He peeled a hundred-dollar bill off his roll and laid it on the bed stand. "That all right with you?"

She looked at the bill, then up at him. "Sure," she said, her voice catching.

"Nobody else, all right?"

"I'm all yours, Slocum."

His mouth quirked up into a grin. "That's my girl," he said, and planted a soft kiss on her forehead. "I'll be back. Sooner or later."

She blushed. "Sooner, I hope."

When he walked down the stairs, Josh and Detroit and the other two were sitting at a table in the otherwise vacant barroom. Josh was staring at his hands, Detroit was keeping an eye on the street, and the other two were engaged in conversation.

One of them, Slocum figured to be the town deputy, on account of the beat-up tin badge on his shirt. He hoped the deputy would be more helpful than the sheriff had been.

Course, that wouldn't be too difficult.

The fourth man wasn't dressed like a cowhand, or even a saddle tramp.

He wore woolen trousers that looked like they'd seen better days, wide suspenders and a red checkered shirt. His jacket, which he'd slung over the back of a chair, was leather, lined with fluffy wool. And instead of a regular hat, he wore a black, short-billed cap of some sort. He looked a mite worn around the edges, too.

A haggard Josh looked up as Slocum approached the table and nodded at him. The kid didn't appear as if he'd slept a wink.

"Mornin'," Slocum said, and scraped out a chair.

"I see you got your beauty sleep, Slocum," quipped Detroit.

Slocum grunted.

"These gents are Deputy Bill Clancy and Marcus O'Brien. O'Brien's the biggest man in sheep round these parts."

Slocum nodded. "I remember your name. From the papers. And you, Deputy, look a little familiar to me. Can't place you yet, though."

"Cochise Springs, over to Arizona, Slocum," the deputy said. "Ring a bell?"

It did. He remembered Bill Clancy now. He was older than the boy that Slocum had pulled from Jeb Dalton's line of fire, but it was him, all the same.

"Sure does," Slocum said, grinning. "You've growed considerable."

Clancy returned the smile. "That I have. You ain't changed much, though."

Slocum shook hands with both men, then said, "What can we do for you?"

"Deputy Bill Clancy, here, is a whole lot more helpful than his boss, Slocum," Detroit piped up. "When O'Brien rode in this mornin' to report that one of his men got shot last night, he put two and two together right away."

"Got shot?" Slocum asked, his brow arched.

"Murdered," replied O'Brien.

Slocum frowned and said, "Tell me about it. But tell me over breakfast, up to the café. No disrespect to your situation or your murdered man, but I could eat a fried horse."

Mitcham found himself a flock of sheep within an hour of splitting with the others. He rode his horse back down to the bottom of the hill, tied it to a scrubby bush, then grabbed his rifle and worked his way back up to the crest of the hill on his belly.

As he had suspected, nobody had seen him. It was a good-sized flock, maybe a couple hundred head— or whatever you called sheep, anyway—and there were two shepherds and a couple of dogs with them.

They were taking a break, Mitcham supposed. The dogs were at ease, drowsing in the purplish shade of a paloverde, and the shepherds—one standing, one sitting—seemed relaxed.

A regular pastoral portrait.

Mitcham, however, wasted no time. He brought up his rifle and took careful aim on one of the shepherds. He squeezed the trigger, the shot echoing in his ears.

But the men were a long way off. Before the first shepherd had time to fall, before Mitcham's first slug even reached its target, he swiftly moved the barrel of the rifle to the left and sighted down on the second man. Again, he pulled the trigger.

Mitcham was far enough away that the men hit the ground, one after the other, before the dozing dogs heard the gunshots.

When they did, a second later, they both leapt to their feet. One began to bark, his hackles raised and his head turned toward Mitcham's hiding place, the source of the shots. The other ran immediately to the first downed shepherd and nosed at him pitifully.

Mitcham shot that one next.

Then he shot that goddamn barking dog.

Sheep were incredibly stupid, he thought with disgust as he got to his feet and started down toward the flock. All they'd done was skitter a little when the damned dog barked, but they hadn't hightailed it.

Not like cattle at all. Cattle would have hightailed it straight off. Hell, they'd be heading for the next county.

This was going to be easy.

He patted his pocket to make certain he'd remembered the extra boxes of ammunition. He had.

Slowly, he got to his feet and set off, down the hill and toward the flock. He wondered: Just how many sheep could a fellow kill with one slug if they happened to line up right?

He was going to find out.

16

Slocum pushed away his pillaged plate at about the same time that Bill Clancy did. After scrubbing his mouth with his napkin, Slocum said, "The sheriff going to do anything about this, Bill?"

Bill Clancy, who had relayed everything he knew, shook his head solemnly along with O'Brien.

"I know Sheriff Davis," Clancy said. "He ain't gonna take no action till he just about has to. And he ain't gonna figure that one dead Mexican—no offense, Mr. O'Brien—is actionable in any way, shape or form. He's just gonna say it was some stranger, ridin' through, and he don't have no jurisdiction."

O'Brien nodded, and the look on his face was pure disgust. "Just what I figured. Got any ideas, Slocum? Mr. Detroit? I'd sure like to hear one or two. I'd like to hear anything, along about now."

Detroit, who was wiping the last of his fried eggs from his mustache, asked, "Well, what's he gonna consider actionable? Suppose somebody starts killin' sheep? Or more shepherds?"

"There'll be some kind of excuse," Clancy said, his mouth set into a line. "Either the sheep will have died from naturally occurrin' bullet wounds or poison, or the shepherds will. I think you can just about figure that this is somethin' that's got to be taken care of outside the law. Unless you count one town deputy. Course," he added, with a hint of a smile, "it'll probably get my butt fired."

Slocum cocked a brow.

"There are other towns," Clancy added. "Other jobs."

"And other sheriffs," Detroit added.

O'Brien, arms crossed over his chest, nodded his head.

"How many men can you count on, O'Brien?" Slocum asked. O'Brien hadn't offered any information along those lines, and it had Slocum curious. A little nervous, too.

"A good question," O'Brien answered. "Most of the ranchers around here would rather not have trouble. They'd rather avoid it to the extent that if it looks like things are going toward cattle, they'll get rid of their sheep. If it looks like sheep, they'll get rid of their cattle. When I first came to this valley, I met with a little resistance. You'd expect that. But things calmed down soon enough. What disturbances there were, I believe, gave them a gullet-full."

"Great," muttered Slocum. "So what help we can count on is zero. But if what you're sayin' is true, then Thane can't count on any from his neighbors, either. Just the help that he hires."

O'Brien nodded. "This is true."

Josh, who had been as quiet as a church mouse with a hangover all morning, piped up, "Well, all we know is that he's hired one man. Mitcham. Right?"

"Only probably," said Detroit, signaling the waiter for more coffee.

"That's right," Slocum said. "I'd put my money on more men. He's bound to have hired at least two or three. Just in case."

"But still," Josh said with a hopefulness that was a little out of place, "we're more than them, ain't we? Thane'll have men, but O'Brien's got men, too."

"They're shepherds, Josh," O'Brien said quietly. "Not gunmen."

"Oh, yeah," Josh said, hanging his head. "Suppose they ain't much good for anything except birthin' lambs and such."

Slocum made a mental note to have himself a word or two in private with Josh. Something was going on with that kid, and it was more than just nerves.

He picked up his coffee cup and drained it. Setting the cup back in its saucer, he said, "Well, this next will be the hardest part. We've just gotta wait to see what Thane does next."

O'Brien's brows went up. "Wait?"

"We go riding out to Thane's place like a bunch of avengin' angels, we're likely to get massacred," Slocum replied. "We got to wait until we know just who it is he's after."

O'Brien opened his mouth to speak, but Slocum cut him off. "I know and you know and everybody at this table knows," he said, "but there's a difference between knowin' something and provin' it. Plus, I'd hate to send Clancy here off on a fool's errand."

"Huh?" said the young deputy. "What you talkin' about?"

"Tell you later," Slocum said. He lounged back in his chair and proceeded to roll himself a quirlie. "When—and if—the time comes."

He didn't say so, but he was fairly certain that time was coming.

And soon.

Slocum didn't have long to wait. At about three o'clock that afternoon, long after O'Brien had set off for home and Clancy had gone back to his office and Josh had gone off God-knew-where, Slocum and Detroit were sitting out front of the saloon, smoking and whittling to pass the time, when an agitated rider blew past them, galloped up the road and came to a halt in front of the jail.

Slocum immediately dropped the wood he'd been whittling into shavings and got to his feet. Detroit did the same, and followed him, at a jog, toward the sheriff's office.

When Slocum pushed open the door, the distraught rider was already pouring out his story. Which seemed to be having little effect on Sheriff Davis.

Which surprised Slocum not at all.

". . . and they just killed 'em!" the man was saying, gesturing wildly with his hands and arms. "Killed 'em all!"

"Now, Jess," Davis, replete in his stovepipe hat,

began calmly, "you know there's nothing I can do, 'less you seen the actual killin's." Then he looked toward the door, and finally his face took on an expression other than boredom. It was anger.

"What the hell do you two want?" he demanded.

"Just like to hear this feller's story from the start," Slocum snapped. "We warned you somethin' like this was gonna happen. What was it?" he asked, turning toward the rider. "Somebody kill another sheep man?"

"Two of 'em!" the man said, tears welling in his eyes. "Two good men and the dogs and all the sheep, save five that scattered. They was like my brothers, Tom and Paco were. They was about all we had, outside of a few milk cows and a dozen head of cattle. Who'd do this, mister?"

"Were they grazing on your property?" Grover Detroit asked.

"No," cut in Sheriff Davis curtly. "They was out on the open range. It ain't my jurisdiction. And it ain't none'a your business."

Slocum took a quick look around. "Where's Clancy?"

"Never you mind where he is," Davis snapped. "Just get outta my office and get on with your business, whatever it is, before I arrest you for loitering."

"You can arrest a man for loiterin', but not for murder?" yelped the rider.

"You get out, too, Jess Harper," Davis said, rising. "Don't come back here again unless you actually see somebody doin' something. And unless it happens on your private land. Got that?"

Jess Harper, the rider, spat on the floor, then pushed between Slocum and Detroit on his way out the door. Slocum and Detroit followed.

Jess was halfway on his horse before Slocum got to him.

"Hold up, there," Slocum said.

"We're wantin' to help," Detroit added.

"I know who done this," Jess said. His tears were threatening no longer. They had emerged, and were flowing freely down his cheeks. "It was Thane's men. He's been a thorn in our sides for years, and now he's wiped us out. I gotta go home and tell my big brother."

Suddenly, Jess dropped his reins and covered his face with his hands. "Dear Christ!" came his muffled words. "What are we gonna do now? Tom and Paco, out there dead on the ground, and the dogs, too! And all them sheep!"

Detroit put a comforting hand on the boy's leg and said, "Hang on, kid. We're here to help."

"What help can you be?" Jess said, suddenly dropping his hands. "I don't even know you! Who are you, anyway?"

"Grover Detroit," Detroit said.

"And my name's Slocum," said Slocum. "Us and a feller name of Josh Quaid been trackin' a no-good piece of business all the way from Arizona. Goes by the name of Jack Mitcham. We figure he's signed on with this Thane character for the duration."

"He's a gunfighter?" Jess asked.

"He's more like hell for hire," said Slocum. "You don't want to mess with him."

"But we will," Detroit said with a grin.

Slocum turned toward him. "You don't have to be so goddamn happy about it, you know."

"I take comfort from the small things, Slocum," Detroit replied.

Jess just looked confused.

Slocum turned his attention back to the young man on the horse. "You go on home, tell your brother. You know where Marcus O'Brien lives?"

Jess looked at him like he was a lunatic. "Sure. Everybody does."

"All right," said Slocum. "You and your brother meet us there tonight, round about six or seven. That ought to give you time to bury your dead."

Jess let out a long sigh, but seemed more hopeful than he had in the ten minutes Slocum and Detroit had known him. At least, some of the panic, if not the pain, was easing from his face.

"Seven," he said, grimly. "We got a lot of holes to dig."

"Fair enough, Jess," Slocum replied. "Now get going."

The young man nodded, then wheeled his mount and cantered off down the street.

Detroit turned to Slocum. "Well?" he said. "What now?"

"Now we go find our young deputy friend," Slocum replied. "And Josh, too. Don't know where the hell that kid could have got to!"

While Detroit went to ask around town for Deputy Clancy, Slocum went straight to the livery. He checked all their horses, determined that Josh had been by earlier in the day, and set off toward the hotel. He figured he'd try there first for the boy.

As it turned out, he was right. After his second knock, Josh opened up the door. Slocum bulled his way past and into the room. He grabbed the only chair in the room, twisted it around and sat down on it backward. He splayed his arms across the top of the backrest and thumbed back his hat.

"Far as I can see, this room ain't more than nine feet to a side. Why'd it take you so long to answer the door?"

Josh shrugged.

"All right, Josh," Slocum said, but in a softer tone of voice. "What is it? Something's botherin' you. I think I know what it is, but I want to hear it from you. It'll help if you just say it out."

Josh just stared at him.

"I'm waitin'," said Slocum.

Josh slumped down on the bed and stared at the opposite wall. "I'm scared, all right?" he practically shouted. Then he got control of himself, and added, "I'm scared I'm gonna get myself killed, and then there won't be nobody but my idiot cousin to carry on the family name in Iowa. I'm scared to die like my brothers did. And I'm scared to live on, knowin' that at the last minute, I turned yellow."

If the kid was waiting for somebody to stand up and applaud at his grand speech and his talent for self-understanding, he was going to have to wait a whole lot longer. Because Slocum just said, "Is that all?"

Josh's head snapped around. "What do you mean, 'Is that all'?" he demanded angrily. "Ain't that just about everything? Livin' and dyin'?"

"It ain't livin' and it ain't dyin', Josh," Slocum said quietly. "Those are just givens. Everybody lives and everybody dies. It's how you do both that counts."

Slocum and Josh—who was feeling some better after a long talk with Slocum—were headed toward the saloon for a beer when Detroit flagged them down from the other side of the road. With him was the deputy, who looked a little rumpled around the edges.

They waited for Deputy Clancy and Detroit to cross over, and Detroit opened up with "Nobody told me that he works nights and sleeps days."

"You should have figured it out," mumbled Deputy Clancy, as if he'd already said it several times before. He rubbed at his eyes, then poked a thumb toward Detroit. "He said you wanted to talk to me, Slocum."

This was all news to Josh, who had been intent on discussing his own problems. He asked, "Why?"

"Didn't you bring the boy up to date, old buddy?" Detroit asked.

They started walking up the street again, and turned into the saloon. Al waved at them from behind the bar and asked, "Beer all round?"

Slocum nodded, and shepherded them to a table. "Josh," he began, "you can just hang on a second. Let me get this business cleared up with Bill here first."

Josh nodded. It was fine with him. He guessed.

Slocum turned toward the deputy. "Bill, a feller named Jess Harper came thunderin' into town this afternoon."

"I know him and his brother, both," Deputy Clancy broke in. "Good men, the both of them."

"Said that somebody killed two of his hands. He'd found 'em out on the open range," Slocum sent on. "Sounded like a real massacre. Killed the men, killed the dogs, and killed all the sheep but four."

"Five," corrected Detroit.

"Five," echoed Slocum. "The sheriff wasn't too keen on doin' anything about it."

Deputy Clancy nodded slowly. "I figured as much. I can just hear him."

"Right," said Slocum. "So I want you to take yourself to the telegrapher's office and send a wire to the territorial marshal's office. Address it to Steve Fuller. Tell him there's a range war brewin', and that I'm here and so's Detroit. Tell him to come, and bring help."

"Why don't you wire him yourself?" Clancy asked dubiously.

"Because a deputy sheriff's gonna have more clout

with the territorial marshal than just some citizen, that's why," Slocum answered. "Then, after you do that, I want you and Detroit to make the rounds of all the ranchers you think might be even a little bit helpful. Tell 'em about the Harpers' men and their livestock. Tell 'em about O'Brien's man. And then tell 'em to be at O'Brien's place tonight, around seven."

"Meeting?" Clancy asked.

Slocum nodded.

"It's already started, then," said Josh, and felt dread opening a hole in the pit of his stomach.

Slocum nodded again. "Yeah," he said, and his face was stone. "It's started."

17

"Find anything?" Siler asked Blackfoot. The two men had met up fifteen minutes ago, and Siler, who couldn't stand it anymore, was the first to speak.

Blackfoot, never frivolous with words—or anything else, so far as Siler could tell—simply said, "No."

Siler couldn't seem to shut himself up, however. He said, "Passed a whole lot of cattle, but no sheep. Maybe we should try farther north tomorrow. Wonder how Mitcham did."

Blackfoot simply grunted, and Siler gave up on conversation. He was greatly looking forward to getting back to Thane's place and having some dinner. All he'd had for his lunch was a chunk of jerky and some warm water from his canteen.

He was about to tell Blackfoot that he was going on back, and that Blackfoot could wait for Mitcham or not—he didn't care. But just before he could say it, they spied Mitcham coming toward them over the plain. He didn't seem to be in much of a hurry. He was just casually jogging along, so far as Siler could tell.

"Wish he'd hurry the hell up," Siler muttered. "I'm hungry enough to eat a bear."

"They're good if you have enough onions," said Blackfoot, who didn't bother to look at him. His eyes were on Mitcham. "He found sheep," he said with assurance.

"Huh?" asked Siler. "How the hell can you tell? He's still a quarter of a mile out!"

"He rides with satisfaction," said the hatchet-faced Blackfoot, and then he fell silent again. And remained so until Mitcham joined them.

Siler lifted a hand in greeting, although it was half-hearted. Mitcham nodded at him without expression, then rode right past without missing a step or slowing in the slightest. Blackfoot and Siler had to break into a short canter to catch up.

"You find sheep?" Siler asked.

Mitcham nodded.

"How many?"

Mitcham shrugged. "Maybe a hundred. Maybe more. Got five of the suckers with one slug." For the first time, he evidenced a hint of a smile. It gave Siler the collywobbles.

"You shot a hundred sheep?" he asked, his voice a little higher pitched than normal.

"Round about," said Mitcham. He hadn't looked at Siler once. He just kept his eyes straight ahead, at their path. "Got two sheepdogs and a couple'a stinkin' shepherds, too. Along with your Mexican last night, Blackfoot, I reckon that oughta get ol' Thane's range war started."

The half-breed grunted in agreement.

It suddenly struck Siler that they weren't getting paid enough for this job.

Not by a long shot.

By seven-thirty that evening, the whole crowd had gathered at O'Brien's house.

As O'Brien had previously warned Slocum, there weren't many of them: just the Harper brothers, Jess and Joe—who looked so alike, even though they were separated by two years, that Slocum figured they ought to wear name tags—and O'Brien, and a scrawny, long-bearded wire of an old man, Tom Cooper.

And Slocum's crew, of course.

Detroit leaned close to his ear. "I think we're in a shit load of trouble, ol' buddy," he whispered. "That Cooper character looks like he couldn't even heft a rifle, let alone fire it."

"There's nothin' wrong with my hearing, sonny," old Cooper snapped defiantly. "Have you know I fought in the War betwixt the States, was a captain in the by-God Confederacy, and I can shoot with the best of 'em. Even with a great big ol' rifle-gun," he added snidely.

Marcus O'Brien appeared with a big coffeepot, held by a dishcloth-wrapped hand. "More coffee, gents?" he said.

Within an hour, Slocum had laid out most of the plan. First, they were to alert everyone to bring their sheep in off the open range, and keep them close.

Detroit allowed that most of the men they'd talked to that afternoon were already in the process of rounding up their stock and bringing them home. The Harper brothers' loss had not been taken lightly, even if most of the sheep men had declined to show up tonight.

Shepherds were to be armed, both with rifles and handguns, and were to operate in either trios or units of four, whenever possible. Slocum figured the more horizons they could keep an eye on, the better.

When O'Brien pointed out that most of the shepherds he knew couldn't hit the broad side of a barn, Slocum suggested that they come over to O'Brien's place, one or two at a time, for a little lesson. He nominated Grover Detroit for the job of instructor.

Detroit groaned softly and rolled his eyes, but made no verbal comment.

"Just remember," Slocum said, "these boys of Thane's are deadly. They'll kill people, dogs, sheep and whatever else stands in their way. Your boys see somebody they don't know ridin' up, tell 'em to shoot first and ask questions later."

Old Cooper looked over at Deputy Bill Clancy, who so far had done nothing but silently sip his coffee.

"You sayin' that, too, Bill?" the old man asked.

"Well, I sure ain't gonna arrest nobody for it," Clancy said matter-of-factly. "Doubt anybody else is gonna, either."

It was obvious that the Harpers and old Cooper

knew he was referring to none other than Sheriff Davis, because they all nodded.

"Next," Slocum said, "Mitcham knows both Josh and me. So I figured that Grover should ride on out to Thane's place, lookin' for a job."

"Why me?" Detroit asked. "I thought I was givin' marksmanship lessons!"

"Shit," muttered Slocum. "All right. Josh and me will take care of the shootin'. But you're the only one qualified to go out to Thane's. Scout the territory. If he turns you down, we'll at least know the layout, and mayhap how many other men he's hired. If he hires you—and the bastard bloody well might, seein' as you got a bit of a reputation of your own—then you can work from the inside."

Detroit frowned at him. "I'll tell you what I think of your goddamn plan as soon as I get over bein' miffed by that remark about my reputation."

"Why?" piped up Josh. "Don't he have one?"

"Devil Detroit," whispered old Cooper, and made the sign of the cross over his narrow chest. "You're the one they used to call Devil Detroit, ain't you?"

"Ancient history," muttered Detroit.

"Well, hope it ain't so ancient that somebody out at Thane's place don't remember it," Slocum said.

There was a great deal of whispering between the Harper brothers. Then Jess looked up and asked, "Who's Devil Detroit? We're just farmers. We suffered more than anybody so far, but we don't know that we want to get mixed up with killers." Then, hurriedly, he added, "No offense meant, sirs."

Before Detroit had a chance to answer, Slocum spoke up. "Boys, you're already mixed up with killers, and for certain sure the wrong kind. Don't think of it as fightin' fire with fire. Think of us as a great big ol' bucket of water. A river of it."

"Nice, Slocum," Detroit said thoughtfully. "A nice flood to sweep the place clean. I'll have to remember that."

"Oh, shut up," Slocum grumbled.

After all the sheep men had gone home and Detroit had set out for Thane's place, Josh, Slocum and O'Brien sat out on O'Brien's porch. Slocum and O'Brien were both smoking, while, silently, Josh clutched his coffee cup with bloodless fingers.

"It'll be all right, boy," O'Brien said quietly.

"Yes, sir," Josh replied, in little more than a whisper.

Slocum figured the time had come to get Josh's mind off the general proceedings, and he could only think of one thing that would accomplish that.

"You remember as how I told you about Mitcham—that wasn't his name then—ropin' those Mexicans together and shootin' 'em?"

Josh nodded.

"And you remember as how I told you there was somethin' else I owed Mitcham for?"

"Yeah."

"Well, now I'm gonna tell you what it was that he did," Slocum said.

Lifting his gaze from his coffee mug, Josh stared at Slocum. "I'm listenin'."

Slocum noted that O'Brien, on the other side of Josh, was all ears, too.

"About two, two and a half years back, I was up in Montana, trackin' Leopold Krebs. He was wanted for a couple of murders up in Helena."

He paused, waiting for Detroit to make his usual pithy comment, then realized he wasn't there. He went on with his story.

"Anyhow, I tracked him to his hideout. It was up in the hills and hard to find, but I found it. There was only the one way in, which is why nobody had found it before, I guess. At least, nobody on the side of the legalities. You had to go through all these curlicues in the rock, and I had to get past a lookout posted high up, but I made it. Turned out it was a location that was bein' used by all manner of outlaws, from petty crooks and pickpockets to men like Krebs.

"Anyhow, I was wedged into the rocks far up, lookin' the place over with my spyglass, when I saw somebody I knew."

"Who was it?" asked Josh, who was, by now, sitting forward in his chair.

"It was a U.S. deputy marshal, name of Sam Biggens. Friend of mine. Good friend, as a matter of fact. I figured he was down there workin' undercover, 'cause he used to do a lot of that sort of thing, and for a few minutes I wondered if maybe he wasn't on Krebs's track, too."

"But you say you trailed the murderer Krebs in. Wouldn't you have seen this Deputy Biggens on your way in if there was only the one entrance?" O'Brien asked, transfixed.

Slocum nodded. "That's what hit me next. That he couldn't be after Krebs, because he'd got there before both of us. He looked right to home, as a matter of fact."

He paused to stamp out his smoke beneath his boot, then went on. "Now, Sam Biggens was a friend of mine, like I said. Such a good friend that I had saved his life once upon a time, and he'd saved mine on another occasion. He was a good man, one of the best."

"So what happened?" asked Josh.

"I couldn't hear anything, being so far off and all," Slocum went on. "But all of a sudden Mitcham came out of the cabin, then Krebs. There were a few other fellers hangin' around, but I can say that I wasn't payin' much attention to 'em. Mostly, I was watchin' Krebs and Mitcham and Biggens.

"Krebbs and Mitcham appeared to be havin' some kind of a beef that was about to come to blows. Or bullets. Well, Biggens came over and tried to break it up. Got right between them and then they all started arguin'. They drew quite a crowd. Boys started moseyin' over from the corral and the barn, and more from inside the cabin."

Slocum paused to pull out his fixings bag, and proceeded to start rolling a smoke.

"And then what?" Josh asked. Slocum could see that the excitement on his face had nothing to do with what might happen tomorrow or the next day. He was caught up completely in the story.

Slocum licked the quirlie and stuck in between his lips, then fumbled for a match. Before he could produce one, O'Brien leaned toward him, a lit sulphurtip in his hand.

"Thanks," said Slocum, and drew deeply, then jetted out a cloud of smoke through his nose before he went on again. "Anyhow, things were getting pretty tense down there. And there wasn't a damn thing I could do about it, not without bringin' the whole crowd down on me. I just had to trust that ol' Sam Biggens could talk his way out of whatever it was, and could get those boys quieted down. Hell, I'd seen him do it before. No reason to think that he wouldn't."

He paused. "Except that I hadn't taken Mitcham into account. Now, I'd seen him shoot those Mexicans a few years before. Saw him tie 'em in a row and shoot 'em just to see how many he could kill with one slug, O'Brien."

"That's right," echoed Josh.

"Good Christ," muttered O'Brien.

"I don't think Christ had nothin' to do with it," Slocum said. Behind him, a foolish moth flew down inside the lantern, and they all jumped at the tiny explosion its burning body made.

"It was about as quick as that," Slocum said, jabbing a finger toward the lantern. "All of a goddamn sudden, Mitcham drew. He's fast, and I don't say that about many men. I remember it crossed my mind that he was gonna kill Krebs, and there went my bounty. But instead, he shot Biggens right through the heart. Biggens didn't even have time to skin leather. Then he turned the gun on Krebs, and then on another man back in the crowd who'd been stupid enough to go for his gun. Mitcham got him, too."

"What about the others?" Josh asked.

"Oh, they were all runnin' by then. Some of 'em didn't even bother to snare a horse out of the corral, just headed for the hills on foot. A couple of 'em were comin' my way, so, as much as I wanted to ride down there and plug Jack Mitcham, I chose to skinny back down my hill and get on my horse and just go. Figured I'd find me another time and place when the odds were a little more even. So I owe Jack Mitcham. I owe him a world of grief. For those Mexicans and for Sam Biggens."

Slocum stood up and stretched.

Josh sat there, looking up at him, all goggle-eyed.

"You gonna stay here or come back to town with me?" Slocum asked.

"You're both welcome here," O'Brien offered.

"Thanks, but no thanks," Slocum said. "I'm wantin' to get back to town. And back to Lola, too." He smiled.

"A genuinely lovely girl," commented O'Brien around his pipe stem.

Josh stood up, too. "Reckon I'll mosey on back with you, Slocum."

"Suit yourself."

18

Grover Detroit, having carefully listened to O'Brien's directions, managed to find Thane's ranch even in the dark.

The house was damned big. They'd hung lanterns out on the porch posts, and their row seemed to go on forever. Detroit kept a steady pace as he rode up past the big corral and then the first barn, alert for the sound of rifles cocking in the darkness. This was old stuff to him.

But no such sound was to be heard. In fact, the place looked dead, outside of those lights on the house.

Thane must think mighty high of himself. Or be awful dumb.

Slowly, Detroit rode on up to the house, dismounted and hitched his horse to the rail by the steps. No one was outside on the porch, either, but the lights were lit inside.

Odd. He figured that he should have been met by Mitcham, or one of Thane's other hired guns, if there were any. Which he suspected there were.

But he walked up on the porch and crossed its length unhindered. He raised a hand and knocked on the front door. Not too loud, not too timid, just a good, self-confident rap of the knuckles that hopefully said, "I'm a friendly sort, and I'm here to do you some good."

The door was opened by a Chinaman, of all things.

"What you want?" the little man said. "Who comes to call on Missah Thane so late at night?"

Detroit held back his surprise and tipped his hat. "Evenin'. I'm Grover Detroit, and I hope to have business with Mr. Vance Thane."

"You Grover Detroit?" The Chinaman looked him up and down. "Who Grover Detroit?"

As Detroit nodded, from somewhere back in the house a voice called, "Let him in, please, Chan."

Grudgingly, the servant backed up and held the door wide, saying, "Go through back, through back. To light." He pointed with an impatient finger.

Detroit stepped inside and began to make his way down the hall as Chan, the servant, had indicated.

"Where your manners? Take off hat! Take off hat!" he heard the man behind him hiss, and Detroit obeyed without looking back.

He walked toward the light and the growing sounds of low voices and silverware scraping plates. If they were serving supper, he'd surely come at the right time. He was practically starved to death, having had no supper before he left town, and O'Brien hadn't thought to offer anything except coffee.

The coffee was good, but it would have been better with a steak alongside.

He paused, gave his mustache a last smoothing,

then stepped through the door and into the light.

Although none of it showed on his face, he knew most every man in the room except the fat one at the table's head, who he assumed was Thane himself. Along the far side of the table, he recognized Jack Mitcham from Slocum's description: big, dark, and with that ugly facial scar crossing his eye.

Along the near side of the table sat none other than Latham Siler, a man he'd known for a few years, even liked, once upon a time. They worked together one winter, up in the Dakotas.

He wondered what the hell Siler was doing here, but not for long. As he remembered, Siler was like-able enough so long as you didn't cross him. But the man's weak point was that he'd slit his own grand-mother's throat if the price was right.

Next to Siler sat Trey Blackfoot, a nasty piece of business if there ever was one. Just looking at that long-haired, scraggly bearded, walking hatchet pre-disposed Detroit to what his daddy used to call the collywobbles. He was not surprised to see Blackfoot here. It was just his sort of job.

"Hey, Detroit!" said Siler happily. Half-rising, he waved his chin napkin. "What in tarnation you doin' here?"

"Yes, Mr. Detroit," said the man Detroit supposed was Thane. "What *are* you doing here?"

"Mr. Vance Thane, I presume?" Detroit asked.

"Correct." Thane nodded. "Answer my question, please."

"Heard you was hirin' guns," Detroit said without missing a beat. "And I wondered if you'd want to take me on, seein' as I was headin' down through these parts anyhow."

"Why?" Thane said, without expression.

"Why what?" countered Detroit, although in a friendly fashion.

"Why should I wish to hire you, and why were you headed this way?"

"Well," Detroit lied, "I was actually goin' down to Mexico to see a certain little señorita I know down there. You was on the way. And like I said, I heard you was hirin' guns. No offense to present company, gents, but I'm one of the best."

"That he is, Mr. Thane," interjected Siler. "I seen him shoot a hole straight through a silver cartwheel plenty of times. And he killed Big Bob Candy up Sacramento way. Did it with one shot, too, and from a distance of near a hundred yards. Got him right through the old thinker." He drilled his forehead with an index finger to underscore the point.

Siler must be on the outs with Mitcham and Blackfoot, Detroit thought. Otherwise, he would wouldn't be so eager.

Thane ignored Siler, though, or at least appeared to do so. He said, "And just how did you hear that I was hiring, Mr. Detroit?"

Detroit shrugged. "Some feller in a bar. Figured the lead was worth chasin' down. Rode into town yesterday, had me a little fun, then asked around for directions to your place today."

"It took you all day to ride from town to here?" Thane asked through flabby lips.

"Didn't say I got all the fun outta my system yesterday," Detroit said with a grin.

"Can either of your other men vouch for Mr. Detroit?" Thane asked, looking from Mitcham to Blackfoot.

Mitcham shook his head and threw Detroit a dirty look, but Blackfoot grudgingly said, "I know him. He is fast. Very fast."

Thane sat there for a second, considering, and then he looked back at Detroit. "All right, then. We shall discuss the monetary considerations after supper. I never speak about money over my food."

Thane held out a pudgy hand toward the empty chair next to Mitcham, then called, "Mr. Chan, another plate and service, please!"

"Slocum?" asked Josh. They were traveling back to town slowly, by the light of the moon.

"Yeah?"

"I been thinking. About you sending Grover Detroit over to Thane's, I mean."

"Yeah?" Slocum repeated.

"Well, you said that Mitcham would know you," the kid started, hesitantly. "How would he know you by sight if both times you crossed paths, you were hid back away someplace, and only saw what he was doin'? I mean, you were up in the hills that last time—the one you told us about tonight—and the first time, you said you were pinned down by a hail of bullets."

Slocum nodded. "Good questions, Josh. The reason he knows me on sight is because those two times weren't the total extent of our meetings."

Josh looked at him, waiting.

Slocum sighed. "You ain't gonna rest till you hear it all, are you?"

"Nope."

"All right," Slocum said resignedly. "Last year, in Laramie, Wyoming, he happened to walk into a bar where I was playin' cards and mindin' my own business." Slocum kept his eyes on the trail ahead, not Josh. "Mitcham—who was goin' by the name of Summers then—got kind of rough with a for-hire gal. I've gotta say that I didn't look close enough to recognize him until he slapped her. That made all of us look up."

"And?"

"And, to make a long story short, we got into it. I told him as how I'd seen what he'd done to Biggens and those poor Mexicans, told him I'd been lookin' for him for a long time. The son of a bitch just laughed. That was, until somebody said, 'Easy, Slocum.' Or something like that. Anyway, they mentioned my name. It seemed like he must have heard of me, because he backed down some. Not all the way, though." Slocum paused to dig out his fixings bag.

"What'd you do, Slocum?" Josh demanded. "What happened next?"

Slocum paused in his quirlie rolling and said, "We were about to get into it full force when a couple of yahoos crowned us both. Bang, over the head, then nothin'. I had me a lump on my noggin that was big as a goose egg for a good week and a half. Don't know about Mitcham. He was long gone by the time I came to, and nobody knew which way he went. Either that, or they wouldn't tell me."

"Aw, crud," Josh said in disappointment. "Who cracked you over the head, anyway?"

"One'a the town deputies, as far as I could make out later on. They told me the sheriff knocked out Mitcham." Slocum gave his quirlie a lick, then stuck it in his mouth. "So Mitcham knows me, all right. And he knows why I'm after him."

He struck a lucifer, and gold washed up over his face as he lit his smoke. He shook out the match, then tossed it aside. He pulled his jacket a little closer. It was getting damned cold out here.

"Course," he said, "I ain't exactly been hot on his track this past year. I got jobs to do, people to see, like that. But I been keepin' an eye out. For him, and for several others that you don't need to know about."

"And then you ran into me," Josh said.

"More like the other way round, boy," Slocum said

with a smile. "As I recollect, you were the one who
shot me in the arm."

In the moonlight, Josh flushed, then unconsciously
rubbed his head.

"That scalp wound healin' all right?" Slocum
asked. And when Josh turned his head and opened his
mouth, Slocum cut him off with a wink.

Josh grinned.

The hired guns slept in the house. There were no
hands on the place except for Mr. Chan, as the cattle
had been driven far north to greener pastures. Thane
liked to keep his guns close, even when they were
sleeping. Especially tonight.

At least, that was what Thane was telling Detroit.

Thane had dismissed the other men, who were loitering out on the porch. Detroit could see their shadows occasionally crossing the windows.

Detroit himself was standing in the center of the
front parlor, feeling like a kid who'd been called up
in front of the class for throwing spit wads or dipping
some little girl's pigtails in his inkwell. He half-
expected Thane to rap his knuckles with a ruler. The
man appeared to have the audacity to try, anyhow.

Mr. Vance Thane had a way about him, there was
no doubt. But it was more mysterious than imposing,
which was what Detroit suspected he was striving for.
He didn't quite pull it off, though, at least so far as
Detroit was concerned.

He just made Detroit curious.

"So, you're expecting reprisals?" Detroit asked amiably. "For whatever it was that old Mitcham pulled off this afternoon. You were hintin' around about it all during supper. And I heard about some sheep man's hired hand gettin' himself killed during the night. Reckon one of your hired guns is responsible for that, too. Am I right?"

"Yes. And the reprisals are expected sooner or later, in one way or another," the fat man answered. He poured himself a large brandy. He didn't offer one to Detroit, so Detroit simply stepped over to the little built-in bar and helped himself.

He swirled the brandy under his nose. "Good stuff," he said.

Thane merely blinked twice in what appeared, if you used your imagination, to be umbrage, and then he simply stared at Detroit.

Detroit sat down, legs stretched out in front of him, the brandy glass in his hand. He gave his mustache a stroke.

"I've got a pretty good picture of what you're up to, here, Mr. Thane," he began. "How you want to get rid of the sheep and all. So now we get to the important part. How much you payin' for this job?"

As he took his leave and stepped through the foyer, Detroit could hear somebody pacing nervously out on the porch. Siler, he figured. He imagined that Siler was really hating Mitcham and Blackfoot by this time. Both of them were quiet as the tomb unless provoked, and Siler would talk your ear off at the drop of a hat.

Besides, Detroit had gotten the distinct feeling that Mitcham, along with Blackfoot, pretty much thought he was cock of the walk. That wouldn't set too well with a man like Siler, who talked a big game—and came through, most of the time—but was secretly insecure.

By the time Detroit let himself out and closed the door behind him, Siler had paced his way clear down to the far end of the front porch.

Detroit settled his hat on his head and nodded at Blackfoot, who was sitting on a nearby bench, whittling. Siler started to sprint back up to Detroit's end, then seemed to think better of it and held himself down to a slow saunter.

Detroit looked up. "Well, Siler," he said amiably, "I guess I'm part of the staff now." He looked around. "Where's Mitcham?"

Blackfoot answered before Siler had a chance.

"Patrolling," the half-breed said, his whittling knife in one hand and the mostly finished wooden chain in the other. He stood up and folded his pocketknife then carefully set his whittling down on the bench.

"Now I go, too," Blackfoot said without expression, although those eyes of his were piercing. He was one nasty piece of business, and Detroit figured that if Siler would kill his grandma for a dollar, Blackfoot would do the same for a three-cent nickel.

Blackfoot continued, "You two stay here. Keep

your eyes open. Thane wants two men on the house all the time from now on."

Both Siler and Detroit watched as the Indian effortlessly jumped down off the porch and headed toward the barn.

"Real joy-boy, ain't he?" Detroit asked, and Siler laughed.

"Good to see you, Grover," Siler said. "Real good. These yahoos don't talk much."

"And you were always one for the gab, weren't you?" Detroit said with a grin. "You still carry them playing cards every damn place you go?"

Siler said, "Sure!"

It was fair pitiful, Detroit thought, how eager this fellow was for somebody to just pay attention to him.

"Well, bring 'em down here by the lantern," Detroit said. "Let's have us a game."

19

After Slocum and Josh rode back into town and settled Tubac and Stoney at the livery, they dropped by the café and had themselves some supper.

Slocum was relieved to see that Josh was acting more like himself. At least, he fairly inhaled his pan-fried potatoes and onions and roast beef, and ordered two desserts.

The fear—at least, the unreasoning, paralyzing fear—had gone out of Josh. There was still some fear in there, but it was the healthy kind.

If the kid didn't have the sense to be afraid of what they were doing, and to understand the consequences of it, Slocum wouldn't want him riding along with him and Detroit.

Neither did he want Josh along if he really didn't want to be there.

But it seemed that he'd struck a good middle ground in the kid. He smiled to himself, and scooped up the last of the peas on his plate.

"You got a tapeworm or somethin'?" he joked, indicating Josh's second piece of pie. The first one had been apple. This one was cherry.

"Nope," answered Josh around a mouthful of food. "Just feel like eatin'. For a change."

"Well, don't hold back on my account," Slocum said, smiling. "Dinner's on me."

"Again?"

"Again. See, there's somethin' I ain't told you."

Josh hoisted a brow. "And what's that?"

"There's a reward on Mitcham."

Slocum had expected a shout of *What?!* from Josh, or at least a look of surprise, but all he said was "Yeah, I know."

"You know?" Slocum thundered, and every other head in the café—which was exactly three—turned toward him. He lowered his voice and hissed, "And you didn't say nothin'?"

Josh blinked a couple of times, then quite innocently said, "Well, you didn't tell me either, y'know."

Slocum frowned. "What'd you plan on doin'? Were you gonna just take the money and run, once we brought Mitcham down?"

Josh appeared hurt, and Slocum wished he could take his last words back. But it was too late.

"No," said Josh, "I was gonna split it with you. Course, now we got to split it three ways, what with Mr. Detroit comin' in and all."

Slocum just shook his head. "Josh, I'm sorry. But you beat everything, you know that?"

Josh forked another bite of pie into his mouth. "I been told," he mumbled around it. He chewed and swallowed, then asked, "Slocum? How you figure Mr. Detroit is doin' out there? I ain't mentioned it, but it's been preyin' on my mind."

"Been wonderin' the same thing, Josh," Slocum replied. Absently, he fiddled with his fork. "Can't help but worry a little bit. But don't you fret none. If anybody in this blue-eyed world can take care of himself, it's Grover Detroit."

Suddenly Slocum grinned wide. "Right about now, I imagine Detroit's about as cozy as a bluebottle fly in a bucket of hog gizzards."

Grover Detroit sat his horse, alone, atop a hill out on Thane's south range. He had played far too many hands of poker with Siler, he was sleepy, he was cold, and it had just started to dust snow.

He pulled his hat down lower over his brow and hugged himself with gloved fingers. His horse, oblivious, dozed beneath him as the snow softly and slowly blanketed them both.

It was past midnight. Blackfoot and Mitcham had ridden in about eleven and sent Siler and him out to keep watch. They were supposed to ride back in at about four and wake the other two again. Siler had gone off in the opposite direction to the one Detroit had, shouting amiably, "Gonna be colder than the balls on a brass monkey tonight!"

Well, Siler couldn't play cards worth shit—Detroit had come out twenty-three bucks and change ahead, even with a measly nickel limit—but he knew his weather.

Maybe not well enough, though. Brass monkey didn't begin to cover it.

Course, he supposed it wouldn't have seemed so cold if he hadn't spent the last two winters where it was warm. The Salt River Valley in Arizona Territory one year, and southern California the other, to be exact.

Mayhap he should have spent the last few years up in Minnesota or Montana. Then this would have seemed like light jacket weather.

As it was, his heavy jacket felt about as heavy as a cotton shirt.

"I don't know what I'm doin' sittin' out here with no cover," he muttered. "Hell, I know damn well ain't nobody gonna come to call on Thane tonight!"

He took off his hat and slapped the light, dry snow from it, then crammed it back down over his head. He picked up his reins, thus waking his horse, which then shook from head to tail.

That got Detroit's blood going again, at least a little bit.

"I'll bet it's not this cold down in town," he grumbled as he reined the horse down toward a small glade of trees, and therefore some shelter. "I'll just betcha Slocum's nice and warm, all tucked in with a fire going and that pretty Lola gal cooing in his ear. Goddamn his ugly ass, anyhow!"

Slocum rolled off Lola for the second time that night and, putting his arm about her shoulders, hugged her close.

She, in turn, rolled toward him and pillowed her

head on his chest. She took his hand and placed it over her breast: slick with sweat, soft and pillowy. He gently rolled the nipple between his knuckles.

"You sure you don't want to stay around forever?" she asked softly. And then she caught herself, adding quickly, "I didn't mean that like it sounded, Slocum. I mean . . ."

A deep chuckle rumbled out of him. "I know what you meant, Lola honey. Don't worry your pretty head about it."

He had just about decided what he wanted to do with a good chunk of his share of the reward. That was, if Mitcham—or somebody like him—didn't get him first. He wanted to get Lola out of the whoring trade for good and all.

It wasn't like she'd chosen to get into it. Others had chosen it for her by force.

And it wasn't as if she seemed to like it. At least, with anybody else but him. She'd made that pretty damned clear.

He figured a couple thousand dollars would let her get back east, where nobody had ever heard of Cholla, New Mexico Territory. She could buy a house and fix it up nice, and maybe get herself a real job, maybe teaching school again.

She was awful sweet. He would have bet that she was an angel with kids.

The West was a hard place for women like her.

Well, it was a hard place for any woman, especially a woman on her own.

But still, he didn't say anything. He didn't want to get her hopes up. There were a lot of sticks that could get caught in the wagon wheel spokes before this thing was over.

He kissed the top of her head and whispered, "Let's get some sleep, baby."

She sighed happily and snuggled closer, and placed her hand over his, hugging it to her breast. Her long-lashed eyes fluttered closed.

For Slocum, slumber didn't come so easily, though. Despite what he'd told Josh, he was concerned about Grover Detroit. But there was nothing anyone could do to find out what was going on, save ride out there and get themselves shot.

He fretted over it for about a half hour before he, too, gave in to sleep.

Something jarred O'Brien from his sleep.

At first, in that half-dreaming, half-waking state, he thought he was again a lad in New England, that he was up in the loft with Mary-Elizabeth Tucker, the preacher's daughter, and that his father had just walked into the barn and knocked over a rake.

Accordingly, he froze and clapped his hand over Elizabeth's mouth to cover her careless giggles.

But then the sound came again, and he realized that it was no rake he heard, that he was a grown man in his own house, and that the pretty, bow-shaped mouth he was covering belonged to his spare pillow.

He put on his slippers and snatched up his robe,

quickly shrugging into it. Hollering, "Hold your horses!" he made his way through the chilly house to the front door.

He already had it halfway open before he had the presence of mind to grab for his rifle.

But there was no need.

Standing out on the porch, stamping his feet and beating his gloved hands on his upper arms, stood Grover Detroit.

He opened his mouth to speak, but O'Brien hurriedly pulled him into the house before he had a chance. "Good God, man!" he exclaimed. "Have you no idea what time it is?"

"It's nearly three goddamn o'clock in the morning," Detroit said, going immediately to the dying fire and feeding it several logs.

"Take care!" said O'Brien, swatting at the sparks that Detroit's enthusiasm was throwing out over the floor. "You trying to set my parlor on fire?"

"S-sorry," said Detroit. He squatted, and held his hands so close to the blaze that they were practically in it. "It's goddamn cold out there and I'm just about turned into an icicle. Well, howdy, dog."

Only then did O'Brien realize that RJ hadn't barked, hadn't made a sound, not while Detroit was riding up, not while he was pounding at the door. Right at the moment, RJ was nuzzling up to Detroit like he'd known him all his life.

Now, RJ had been in the room when he and Slocum and Detroit and the others had their meeting earlier that evening, but generally, knowing somebody and liking them were two completely different things to the dog.

O'Brien trusted his dogs, though. And right at that moment, for the first time, RJ was showing such faith in Grover Detroit that he thought that perhaps things would be all right, that everything could be on an even keel once more.

"Nice dog," Detroit said, ruffling RJ's fur. "Meant to tell you before. What's his name?"

"RJ," O'Brien answered.

Detroit didn't look at him. "Awful nice dog," he repeated. "Awful nice."

"Would you like a cup of coffee?" O'Brien asked, automatically heading for the kitchen.

"Yeah," Detroit answered, still petting the dog. "I got just enough time to down a cup and bring you up to date before I gotta head on back to Thane's."

20

Deputy Bill Clancy left the sheriff's office a little after dawn and took himself up to the café to get some dinner.

Or breakfast, depending on how you looked at it. He had a couple of hours to kill before the telegrapher's office opened, anyhow.

He almost stopped at the saloon to get Slocum, but the door was locked, Al apparently not being up yet, and Lola's curtains were drawn. He figured he'd best leave well enough alone. At least for a while.

Al got real crabby when you woke him out of a sound sleep.

Clancy had no more than placed his order—five eggs, sunny side up, biscuits and gravy, a half-rasher of bacon and coffee, black—when he saw O'Brien riding past, out on the street.

He leapt up and ran outside, waving an arm. "Hey, Marcus!"

O'Brien reined in the horse and turned it around. "Morning, Bill. It was you I was looking for, anyhow."

"C'mon in the café, then," Clancy offered. "I just ordered my breakfast."

"Don't mind if I do."

Once O'Brien had hitched his horse to the rail and settled in at Clancy's table, he ordered a cup of coffee and took off his jacket.

"That all you gonna have?" the deputy asked. "Just coffee?"

"Had breakfast before I left the house," O'Brien replied. "We got some snow out there. Imagine it'll be melted off before too long."

Deputy Clancy checked out the window, just to be sure he wasn't more asleep than he realized. He shook his head. "Nothin' here. Not a flake."

"As usual," O'Brien said. "And what's on Sheriff Davis's mind today?"

"Same as usual," Clancy replied. "Nothin'. He's still sayin' that your Julio was killed by somebody passin' through. And anything that happens out on the range, even when it's two men gettin' killed? Still not his jurisdiction. I'm thinking that I'm workin' for the wrong man. Course," he said, shrugging, "there ain't nobody else to work for round here."

Just then, the waiter began bringing their orders. O'Brien sat in silence for a few minutes, until the man was done unloading his tray—practically all of it in front of Clancy—and then he said, "Hungry?"

"Damn straight," replied Clancy, without expression. He tucked his napkin into his collar and picked up his fork in one hand and a thick strip of bacon in the other. "So, what'd you want to see me about?" He jammed the bacon in his mouth and, chewing, asked, "Anything more happenin' out there?"

"Grover Detroit came knocking on my door at about three this morning," O'Brien said.

Clancy, his mouth now full of biscuits and gravy, nodded. "He got in with Thane all right, then? Slocum figured as how he would."

"Yeah. I've got a message from him for Slocum. He awake yet?"

"Don't know," said Clancy. The eggs were done just right, for a change. He peppered them liberally, then stuffed one in his mouth whole. He chewed, smiling, then swallowed. After a drink of coffee, he said, "Went by the saloon, but it was locked up for the night." He forked up another egg and wrapped his lips around it.

O'Brien hadn't touched his coffee mug yet. He just sat there, looking on in seeming amazement as Clancy chewed.

"Well, hell," he said, finally, and craned back around toward the waiter. "Could you bring me a plate of bacon and eggs?"

He turned back toward Clancy, saying, "Gotta do something to pass the time while you're working your way through that giant wad of food. I'm surprised you aren't as big as a house, Bill."

Clancy grinned at him and kept on eating.

Slocum opened one eye and frowned.

He slid out of bed, hollered, "Just a second, goddammit!" and pulled on his britches and strapped on his guns. "That your voice I hear out there, Bill

Clancy?" he called as he slid into his shirt.

Behind him, Lola was putting on her robe. Damn shame, if you asked him. She was a pure beauty when she was naked. Well, when she was dressed, too, but being in the nude really put the capper on it.

"Yeah," shouted Deputy Clancy through the door. "It's me, and O'Brien's here, too. He's got a message for you. From Detroit."

Slocum yanked open the door and pulled Clancy into the room by his collar. "Why don't you tell everybody?" he hissed.

O'Brien walked through the door, covering a chuckle. "I think it's too late, Slocum," he said.

"Oh. Sorry," Clancy said.

"Don't suppose you remembered to pick up young Mr. Quaid on your way, did you?" Slocum asked.

"They did," said a groggy voice from the hallway. Josh walked through the door, his face still puffy from sleep. He yawned, then rubbed at his eyes.

"Mornin', Slocum," he said. "Mornin', Miss. Excuse my manners."

"Good morning, Josh," Lola said. "And no excuse is necessary. It's awfully early."

Slocum sat down in the overstuffed chair and started to pull on his boots. "Well? What's the message? How'd he get it to you, anyway?" he asked O'Brien.

"Is it all right to talk?" O'Brien asked, and indicated Lola with a slight movement of his head.

"Yeah," Slocum said, and stomped on the first boot to get his foot settled all the way down.

"Well," O'Brien said, "he turned up at my place round about three in the morning. He said Thane took him on and seemed happy to have him. The more the merrier, you know? He's got three other guns out there besides Detroit. The first is Mitcham, but then you knew that. Said that Mitcham claimed responsibility for those murders and the sheep massacre yesterday. The son of a bitch thought it was funny, damn him."

Slocum grunted, then muttered, "Sounded like his style, all right. Who are the others? Did Detroit know 'em?"

"Yes and no," O'Brien said. "There was a man named Siler that he said he knew from a long time ago."

"Name sounds kinda familiar," Slocum said, pulling on the second boot. "Can't put a face to it right off, though."

O'Brien said, "The other one, the one he didn't know except by reputation, was named Blackfoot."

A quick shiver ran up Slocum's spine. He stopped pulling at the boot. "Half-breed? Tall and skinny with a face like an axe blade?"

O'Brien nodded. "I believe the exact word that Mr. Detroit used was hatchet-faced. He didn't seem too fond of him. Actually, he didn't seem any too fond of any of them."

Then O'Brien's fists clenched at his sides. "He said

this Blackfoot was the cowardly wretch that killed my man Julio."

"Easy, O'Brien," Slocum said. "He'll pay for it. In good time."

The name Siler was vaguely familiar to Slocum, but he'd met Blackfoot once, when Blackfoot tried to kill him. Reese Macleod had put out private paper on him a few years back, because he was pissed that Slocum had made time with his girlfriend, Ida.

Truth to tell, Ida was scared to death of Macleod and welcomed Slocum's attentions. Welcomed them even more when he offered her enough cash to get her out of the territory and far away from Macleod's reach.

Slocum eventually got the whole thing cleared up—after a very long and nearly deadly "chat" with Reese Macleod—but before that, Blackfoot had come hunting for him, for the bounty.

Blackfoot found him, too.

Slocum still bore the scar where Blackfoot's knife has skittered along his ribs. They had fought desperately, and in the end Blackfoot went over a cliff. Slocum nearly did, as well. Slocum had left him for dead—it was an awfully long fall, and Slocum was half-dead himself—but now it seemed that Blackfoot had an exceedingly strong will to live.

At least, he was out at Thane's place, alive and breathing. Damn him.

Slocum pulled his boot the rest of the way on, then stood up and stamped his foot. "That's it?" he asked.

"Just the usual cowhands," O'Brien said. "But Detroit says they're out on the range, with the cattle. It's the other three we've got to worry about."

"No foolin'," said Slocum.

By the time they'd stopped by the telegrapher's so that Clancy could fire off a wire to the territorial marshal's offices and the four of them had ridden out to O'Brien's place, now completely cleared of snow, Slocum and the others had heard the whole story from O'Brien.

Detroit had told him that he didn't know what kind of mischief Thane had planned for them to do today, but he figured there wasn't too much he *could* do, if all the sheep were in off the open range. Detroit figured he'd be waiting for somebody to make the next move.

Silently Slocum agreed with Detroit's thinking, but he figured they ought to be prepared, just in case.

Deputy Clancy retired to O'Brien's guest room to catch a few winks, and Slocum, O'Brien and Josh Quaid, accompanied by the dog, RJ, set off for the Harper spread to find Jess and Joe.

At last, they rode over the crest of a gentle hill. Down in a cup of land below, they saw one of the brothers working the soil in what looked like a big truck patch. The other was nowhere in sight.

"Hey, Jess!" Slocum shouted.

He looked up, squinting, his gun drawn. But when

he saw who had hollered at him, he tucked it back in his holster.

"I'm Joe," he said. "Jess is up to the house. You got news?"

"Let's go find Jess so I only have to say it once," Slocum said. "You know, you boys oughta have your names tattooed on your foreheads or somethin'."

Once the Harper boys were brought up to date, Josh, O'Brien and Slocum, along with the dog, rode on out to Tom Cooper's place and repeated everything they'd told the Harper boys. Slocum was sort of glad that no more men had shown up the night before. He was getting weary of talking.

Cooper mostly grunted, but when Slocum rolled out what he'd come up with in the way of a plan, the old man got a hint of a grin on his face.

"I'd surely like to see that," he said, absently scratching the dog's head. "Be like the old glory days again."

Something kept on bothering Mitcham, although he couldn't put his finger on it exactly. After he woke up that morning, he thought about it a good long time. Something about the little Chinaman and Thane wasn't right.

Hell, it almost seemed like Thane was secretly taking orders from his servant! There was all that muttering in the hall the other day, for instance. Now, he couldn't hear a word they said, but Thane sort of, well, carried himself different when the servant was around.

But that couldn't be right. No white man in his right mind would work for a Chink.

Still, there was something funny about the whole deal.

And that Detroit character bothered him, too. Grover Detroit? What the hell kind of a name was that? He'd been up to something last night, Mitcham would have bet on it.

Blackfoot had told him there were no orders for the day—at least, not yet—so Mitcham busied himself fiddling with his horse and tack and mending that girth strap he'd been meaning to stitch up.

He didn't like these downtimes, and he preferred not to hang out in front of the house with the other men. They weren't worth his salt, anyhow. He wanted some action, like yesterday's.

Five sheep with one shot! Now, that was one for the record books!

Come noon, his growling stomach overcame his misgivings, and he wandered on up to the house. He was right on time, because Blackfoot and the other two were just walking down the porch, toward the front door, and he smelled beef stew. Or something like it.

He shoved Siler out of the way and walked in ahead of him.

As he suspected, Siler, the shitty little stinkbug, didn't retaliate. Snorting derisively, Mitcham walked down the hall to the dining room, his spurs jingling on the polished wood floors.

"Welcome, gentlemen," said Thane, who was already seated. "Let us have some of Mr. Chan's finest beef Beaujolais, and then I will lay out this afternoon's plan for you."

"That'd be fine, Mr. Thane," Siler said.

Goddamn little rabbit. Where'd Thane pick him up, anyhow?

"Pleased," said Detroit, and pulled out a chair.

Silently, the Chinaman began to serve. It wasn't exactly beef stew, but at least it smelled halfway decent.

Mitcham decided to let the Thane/servant thing go for a while, and concentrate on Detroit. Casually, he said, "You musta done quite a bit of ridin' last night, Detroit."

Detroit was helping himself to some of the fancy biscuits on the table. They were shaped funny, Mitcham thought, fat in the middle and skinny on the ends, rolled up all fancy.

"That I did," said Detroit. "You opposed to a man doin' his job?"

"Just seemed strange, your horse all lathered up like that," Mitcham said. "You was still scrapin' the steam off him when I come down to the barn to get ready for my turn."

"Can't scrape steam," Detroit replied calmly. "I was scrapin' sweat off him. What do you care, anyhow? He's my horse."

Siler laughed, and Mitcham shot him a dirty look. He shut up quick enough.

"And seein' as how you're so all-fired interested," Detroit went on, buttering one of those funny biscuits, "once I had him all scraped off, I blanketed him and walked him for about a half hour, till he was all the way dry. That all right with you?" Detroit arched a brow. "Not that I care, mind you."

"Why you stinkin' little . . ." Mitcham went for his side arm, but Blackfoot grabbed his arm before he could reach it.

"Later," the Indian muttered.

"Gentlemen, gentlemen!" Thane said sternly. "We will all get along. I will not have my hired help coming to blows. At least, not amongst themselves. Save it for the sheep men."

Hired help? Thane was lucky that Blackfoot still had a hold on Mitcham's arm, or Mitcham would have plugged him. Hired help, his ass!

"So, Mr. Thane," said Grover Detroit, chewing his goddamn stew. Or whatever it was. "What's your plan for today? I'm rarin' to go! Though I gotta admit I hope it's somethin' more than shootin' Mexicans or sheep. Or even sheepdogs. Personally speakin', I like my opponents to be just a little more on the feisty side."

This time, Mitcham shot to his feet. But before he could clear leather, something happened that he couldn't explain. It was like somebody had simply kicked his legs out from under him, somebody he couldn't see.

He landed on the floor on his ass, next to his over-turned chair.

Siler laughed out loud, Detroit chuckled, and even Blackfoot choked back a snicker of sorts.

"What the hell?" Mitcham said. He twisted his head, looking around him. There was nobody else there but the servant, who stood stoically behind him near the wall, his eyes down, his hands folded.

Blackfoot put a hand down to him, but Mitcham pushed it away. He got to his feet, righted his chair, and sat down in it. By that time, the laughter had mutated into the clearings of throats and a cough or two.

Thane said, "For your own good, calm both your tempers and your needling. And as you can see, Mr. Mitcham, I have other ways of stopping you from killing each other. Mr. Chan is my first line of . . . correction."

Mitcham looked over his shoulder at the Chinaman, who bowed solemnly.

"Once we're finished with this sheep business," Thane went on, every word clear and distinct, "I don't care a whit what you do or upon whom you commit murder. But until then, gentlemen, you are mine."

Thane paused, and his gaze went steadily down one side of the table then traveled up the other, from face to face to face-to-face. At last, he quietly said, "Am I understood?"

21

After lunch, Mitcham rode out with the others. All except for Detroit, that was. Thane wanted him to stay behind and watch the place, and this made Mitcham think that maybe Thane had been listening to him after all, that maybe Thane suspected Detroit was up to some funny business.

Good.

If Mitcham's path had crossed that son of a bitch Detroit's, he probably would have killed him, and that would have got him fired. Thane had been pretty clear about that.

And Mitcham didn't want to piss Thane off until he found out a few things. Like, for instance, where the money was kept. He figured to find that out about the time Thane paid them off. He'd been peeking through the windows, as nonchalantly as he could manage, but he still hadn't a clue.

Once he got paid, he also figured to stick nearby, so that after the others went their on way, he could go back, kill that fat bastard and his Chinaman, and clean the place out.

Then it'd be Detroit's turn.

Mitcham would make it last, too. Detroit would find out that it wasn't smart to mess with Jack Mitcham. Or Sonny Smith. He was considering that for his next name. He'd killed a kid named Sonny Smith over in Texas a few years back, and he'd always remembered the name and liked it.

Mitcham, man of many names, had split up with Siler and Blackfoot, and mulled over all this as he scouted the southern range on his alone. So far, all he'd seen was cattle and a few pronghorn and coyotes. Not a goddamn sheep in sight.

Within three hours, it was pretty damned clear that the sheep men had taken their flocks to private land. The cowards. He'd been hoping for a little more target practice.

But he found none, and at about four o'clock he met up with Blackfoot at their predetermined rendezvous. Siler rode in shortly thereafter.

"Find anything?" Siler asked. He got down off his horse and fiddled with his girth strap. "I come up empty-handed. Found me a passel of steers and a few jackrabbits, but not much else."

Blackfoot grunted. "Same for me."

Mitcham nodded. "Nothin'. Musta taken 'em all onto home range."

"All right," Mitcham said as Siler dropped his stirrup again and stepped back up on his horse. Mitcham checked his guns. "Everybody knows what's next."

Siler slapped his holster and said, "Sure do, sure do."

Blackfoot simply reined his horse around and started off toward the southeast, at a jog.

"Goddamn half-breed," Mitcham muttered beneath his breath. "Always gotta be first."

As per Slocum's instructions, the men had split up.

Josh remained at the Cooper place. Not down in the house, with old Cooper, but up high on a hill with a good view of the land between Cooper's place and the open range. One of the first things Slocum had done when they hit town was to buy the kid a new rifle, and when Slocum had left him, he was sitting on a rock with the rifle across his knees.

Slocum had told him to stay awake and stay alert, and to shoot first and ask questions later.

The boy seemed a tad nervous, but then, he should be, shouldn't he? Slocum figured he was up to the job.

He stationed himself in a similar roost just up the hill from Jess and Joe Harper's place, and sent O'Brien back home to wake up Deputy Clancy and instruct him to keep a similar watch on O'Brien's place. They were all to meet there after dark.

At the moment, everything was peaceful down below. Jess and Joe Harper only had about fifty head of sheep left, which had been separated from the others and grazing under the care of a third shepherd on the ranch while the rest were being slaughtered on the range.

They were up close to the house now, and milled quietly in the corral. Their shepherd sat with them, on the edge of the water tank, head in his hands, his shaggy black and white dog curled at his feet.

Joe had finished in the truck patch, and he and his brother were making a couple of crosses and carefully burning names and such into them with a hot iron. Most likely, they'd haul them out to wherever they'd buried their two men.

They weren't taking them anywhere today, though. When the crosses were completed, the boys placed them reverently in a wagon bed, and then abandoned them for other work.

Along about five, Slocum shrugged into his jacket. He'd put it off as long as he could, but the weather had moved from cool and breezy to downright nippy. He gazed up into a sky the color of a dirty nickel, wondering if it would snow and hoping it wouldn't.

He really didn't expect that Thane's men would try anything so bold as a daylight raid on private property, but then again, look at the men he'd hired.

Maybe the sheriff's choice to look the other way had made Thane bold. Or maybe he didn't have much control over his men. Either way, they might come.

But they probably wouldn't. Slocum figured to have it covered either way.

As he rolled his fifth quirlie of the afternoon, he was figuring another hour, hour and a half, and he'd begin to mosey on up to O'Brien's place. Those boys weren't going to come. Not today. He'd have to make the first move, and he was more than willing to make it.

He was just about to hold a lucifer to the end of

his smoke when he saw movement in the trees opposite, on the other side of the Harper place.

He dropped the quirlie and shook out the match, squinting off into the distance.

Maybe he was crazy. It might have been a pronghorn. Might have even been a mountain lion. But he didn't think so.

He pulled out his spyglass and trained it on the trees where he thought he'd seen something moving.

There it was again!

Just a little speck of something red, moving through the branches.

Riders.

He whistled a birdcall, hoping that at least one of the Harper boys would hear him, and luckily, one did. He couldn't tell which one, but he got his brother into the house, and signaled the shepherd to follow them. The dog tagged at the shepherd's heels, the brush of its tail vanishing inside the little house.

He had to hand it to them. They all went in real casual, just like it was about suppertime and they were all going to sit down and have a quiet meal. Just like he'd told them to.

Careful not to disturb the brush, Slocum moved to lie flat on the ground. His rifle was at his side, and the spyglass was still in his hand.

At last, the first rider came into full view. Slocum didn't recognize him. But he was followed by Mitcham, and then that son of a bitch Blackfoot, which, by default, made Siler the first rider. But Detroit wasn't with them. Why not?

There wasn't much time to think about it. They were quite close to the house, just at the edge of the clearing. They reined their horses in and sat there, looking over the situation.

Slocum put down the spyglass and raised the rifle to his shoulder, waiting.

With any luck at all, they'd come round to the front door and start firing. He figured to catch them in the crossfire. Maybe they could get this thing over with in one shot, so to speak.

He wasn't that lucky, though. Suddenly, they split up, with Blackfoot riding around back of the house and out of Slocum's sight, Siler rounding the corral full of sheep and creeping toward the front, and Mitcham staying to the side, but moving a little closer to the house. Right at the moment, he'd gone behind a chicken coop and was hidden by it.

They were circling the little house like a pack of wolves, and suddenly, Slocum realized why. He saw first one fiery torch, then another, sail up from behind the house to land on its roof. Mitcham, still hidden behind the chicken coop, tossed a third flaming torch through the side window. Below, out front of the house, Siler raised his rifle and waited.

Suddenly, the front door burst open, coughing out a huge billow of smoke.

Slocum did the only thing he could do in the circumstances. He fired once, and Siler dropped before getting off a shot.

He wasn't dead, though, and when the Harper boys and their hand and that black-and-white dog came boiling out of the house about a half second later, the dog went right to Siler and pinned him before he could reach for his gun again.

All three men were armed, and they fired wildly, their smoke-teared eyes unable to see what they were aiming at.

They were also in Slocum's way. He could see Mitcham scrambling onto his horse and looking toward Slocum's hiding place, where the smoke from his rifle fire had probably already given him away. But Slocum couldn't fire again without hitting one of the Harpers or their man.

As it was, he just caught a glimpse of the tail end of Mitcham's horse—and Blackfoot's hat—as they quickly disappeared into the trees.

Behind them, they left a flaming house, three men who were still pointing their guns at nothing and firing, and Siler. Either he'd passed out or the dog had finished him off, because now the dog was just lying there beside the unmoving body, its front feet plastered hard over its nose and ears. It was waiting for all the noise to stop.

Slocum stayed low and did the same.

Less than twenty minutes later, and just as Slocum was hauling what seemed like his thousandth bucket of water from the corral tank, Josh came galloping full tilt into the ranch yard and leapt from Stoney before he come to a complete stop.

"Grab a bucket!" Slocum called, and passed his full pail to Joe, who passed it to Jess, who passed it to the shepherd—whose name had turned out to be Ralph—who threw its contents on the flaming house.

But Josh just stood there.

"Move!" shouted Slocum.

"It's lost," Josh shouted back. "We'd best wet down the barn instead."

Slocum saw that the boy was right. He hollered at the others to change their target. Joe—or maybe it was Jess—stood there a moment, arms at his sides, staring at the roaring thing that had once been his home. And then he seemed to snap back again. Water began to arc toward the barn roof.

Josh busied himself drawing water from the well when the tank was emptied, and it was dark before the men, exhausted, sank down to the cold, hard earth. The house was nearly consumed. Every once in a while there was a soft pop as the paint on a cupboard or a chair exploded, or a louder one when a burning timber made its final fall.

The men were silent. They were too tired to speak, too cold to move.

And Siler had turned out to be alive, after all. He sat, roped to the corral fence, with the dog a few feet away. Each time he tried to move or speak, the dog growled. Siler had given up trying to move—or to protest—hours ago.

At last, Josh Quaid broke the silence. "Anybody see where my horse went?" he asked quietly.

"Over there," said one of the Harper brothers, pointing out into the darkness beyond the corral. "He's just grazin'."

Slocum slowly rose to his feet. He ran a sleeve over his brow, and it came away black. He said, "Go round him up, Josh. We got to get to O'Brien's."

Josh rose like an old, old man, and went off after Stoney.

"Can you fellers keep an eye on him till tomorrow?" Slocum asked, pointing to Siler. "He ain't gonna bleed to death or nothin'. Only winged him in the shoulder."

"More's the pity," mumbled Jess. Or Joe.

Slocum moved toward the corral, where Tubac had been waiting patiently, tied to the fence. Slocum leaned against the saddle for a moment, muttering, "Sorry your dinner's late, old son. 'Fraid it's gonna be a little while longer."

He stood erect, took a deep breath, then tightened his cinch. He swung up on Tubac and waited for Josh to ride up from the pasture. They both went up toward the road, and Slocum called back over his shoulder, "And give Siler a coat or somethin'. I don't want him sneezin' to death before they get a chance to hang him."

22

"Don't let the bastard kick you!" cried one of the Harper boys, and the other one jumped clear just in time to avoid Siler's boot.

One of them got behind Siler and dealt a sharp blow to his wounded shoulder, resulting in blinding pain.

Paralyzed with agony, Siler allowed himself to be dragged into a tiny shed and dropped like a bag of grain. Somebody bound his feet together and tossed a couple of feed sacks over him. Then they closed the door, leaving him in darkness. He heard the latch board drop into place.

Outside, a weary voice said, "I think we should just hang him right now."

Another said, "No, Joe. You heard that Slocum feller. Though I gotta admit it wouldn't bother me much if some of the last of that fire was to find its way over to this old shed." Knuckles rapped at the wall just above Siler's head. "Wood's rotted, anyhow. Wouldn't be much of a loss."

Someone laughed, and Siler shivered. This time, it had nothing to with the weather.

"Didn't Slocum say that this here was the one his

buddy knew? That Mr. Detroit?" asked the first voice, and Siler, in the dark, raised his head.

"Think so," came the reply. "What are we gonna do tonight? Where we gonna sleep? What we gonna eat?"

"Hell," answered the second voice in a sarcastic tone, "there's plenty of mutton from yesterday. I'm too damn tuckered to eat. Ralph, run some'a those sheep in the barn. They'll heat it up for us some, I reckon."

Siler heard the crunch as boots walked away.

He was cold, he was bleeding, he couldn't see anything, and he was hungry, but he sure as hell wasn't going to let those goddamned sheep men hang him.

Or set fire to him.

He heard someone whistle, and realized that the dog had been called into the barn with the men. That was one thing on his side, wasn't it?

And then he laughed bitterly, and the sound of it startled him: startled him all the way back from thoughts of revenge and fear and pain to the reality of what he had to do.

Also, what little time he had to do it in. He only hoped they hadn't put his horse in the barn with themselves and the damned sheep.

First things first.

Slowly, a little at a time, he began to work at his back pocket. Because of the fire, those boys had tied him up quick and forgot to check him for knives and such. That was pretty damned stupid of them, because he had a blade in his back pocket. Unless, of course, one of them had taken it during one of the spells when he was passed out.

He shifted his position a little, and felt the knife's outline press into his hip. Thank God. Man, oh, man, when he got back, Grover Detroit was gonna be in a shitload of trouble. And to think he'd played cards with the double-crossing son of a bitch the whole evening last night, lost more than twenty-three bucks to him!

Well, he thought, smiling in the darkness, *I'll get it back soon enough.*

His fingertips met the edge of his knife and he managed to slip it free. Opening it was a different matter, but at last he accomplished that, too.

As he positioned it against the ropes that held his arms behind his back, and painfully began to work it against the most accessible strand, he began thinking about how Detroit had crossed them. And then, about how Mitcham and Blackfoot sure had taken off in a big hurry out there.

They could have tried to pick him up, couldn't they? Could have made some kind of a show of it, anyway. Hell, they hadn't even shouted at him to see if he was all right!

Nobody gives a shit no more, he thought sadly, and shook his head, which sent a fresh lance of pain burning through his shoulder.

He stopped sawing at the ropes and froze, teeth clenched, until the worst of the pain passed, and then he began to saw again. Using only his good arm, he couldn't get much purchase on the blade, but he was certain he was making some progress.

He ought to be, leastwise. It hurt enough.

Well, when he got out of this shed, somebody was going to pay.

And more than money, that was for sure.

Halfway to O'Brien's place, Slocum suddenly hissed, "Off the path!"

Josh didn't ask questions. He just obeyed. They both rode their horses down into the deep ditches on either side of the road. Slocum was still, and Josh waited.

It wasn't more than a few seconds before he heard what Slocum had seen: riders, galloping toward them. He thought it was two. More than one, anyway.

Probably those two that Slocum said had gotten away back at the Harper place.

His hand went to his gun, and he thumbed the strap off it. What should he do? What would Slocum want him to do? It suddenly seemed to him that he was a pretty damned lousy partner. For Slocum now, and for his own brothers before.

He didn't realize that he'd done it, but he found he'd drawn his gun and was crouched low in the saddle, ready to vault up to the road again. His breath was puffing in ragged clouds from his open mouth.

Wait, he told himself. *Don't be a damned jackass!*

He wasn't certain if he was going to ride at those

coming horsemen or away from them, but he felt about ready to jump out of his skin. He had to do something.

And just when he was about to spur old Stoney in the flanks and let him carry him where he might, the coming riders slowed down. He heard something across the road, a rustling and the sound of a horse scrambling up the side of a ditch, and then he heard Slocum's voice.

" 'Bout time," Slocum said.

"Well, we got worried about you," said O'Brien's voice, and Josh's spine, which had been stiff as a plank, eased. "We came looking, and then we didn't see the smoke until a little ways back up the road. Good God, man, you're a wreck!"

Slocum ignored the comment about his personal appearance and said, "Ain't much now. Just wisps. Reckon you boys were too far down in the valley to see it when it was roarin'."

Josh, who knew he looked as smoke-grimed as Slocum, holstered his gun and reined Stoney up the embankment to the road. He hoped his cowardice didn't show on his face.

Slocum sat there on Tubac, facing Marcus O'Brien and Deputy Clancy. Slocum said, "Thane's boys burnt the Harpers out. We were tryin' to put out the fire."

Deputy Clancy's brows shot up. "How many of 'em?"

"Slocum said there was three," Josh volunteered,

more to see if his voice sounded jittery than anything else. He guessed it didn't, because nobody remarked on it. "All but Detroit. Slocum shot one of 'em."

O'Brien said, "Which one?"

"Latham Siler," Slocum replied. "Just winged him, but he's trussed up and out of commission. The Harper boys promised to hang onto him until tomorrow mornin'."

"They all right? And their man?" O'Brien asked.

Slocum nodded. "As all right as they can be with no house. We saved the barn and the outbuildings, though."

Deputy Clancy huffed out a long, relieved sigh— and the accompanying haze of fog—through pursed lips. "Well, I reckon I'm not fired, after all."

Slocum snorted and grinned.

"Huh?" said Josh.

"He didn't report for his shift this evenin'," Slocum said. "Right, Bill?"

The deputy nodded. "And now I got a real good excuse for not showin' up. Arson on private property, for one. And it sounds like I got me a prisoner." He grinned wide. "Sheriff Davis ain't gonna have no choice but to pay attention now."

Slocum shifted in his saddle, and it creaked audibly. Grimly, he said, "Well, while I'd admire to have a little help from town, I got a feeling it'd still take Davis a good week to get organized enough to start what's got to be finished tonight. Don't figure we've got time to wait for the territorial marshal's men."

Clancy nodded. "You got that right, I reckon. So what we gonna do? Those two have had plenty of time to get back to Thane's place, from what you're tellin' us."

"First, I'm wantin' to shove some supper down my gullet," said Slocum.

Josh said a silent thank-you. If he didn't eat something pretty soon, he thought he just might keel over.

Things like being scared half to death and fire fighting—and the fact that it had started to snow again—tended to take it out of a man, he reckoned. All he wanted, right at the moment, was a warm room to sit in and some dinner to eat. And to put off another one of those scared feelings for as long as possible.

He figured he was lucky he hadn't pissed in his pants.

"Fine," said O'Brien, reining his horse around. "I've got some leftover roast lamb at the house, and bread for sandwiches. You men can eat while we ride."

Great, Josh thought as they started back toward O'Brien's and picked up a little speed. *Just great.*

Blackfoot and Mitcham stood in the parlor before Thane. Detroit sat at the side, hat off and perched on his crossed knee. He was enjoying this.

Thane hadn't raised his voice once—so far, that was—but he'd sure made his displeasure known.

"And you're certain that Mr. Siler is deceased?" Thane was saying.

"Weren't like we had time to sashay over there and hold a mirror under his snoot," said Mitcham. His voice was sounding tighter and tighter and more clipped as the interview went on, and Detroit figured it was going to be entertaining seeing who exploded first. Either way, he was near the window. He guessed he could always jump through it if worse came to worst.

Actually, he was sort of hoping that these jackasses would just kill each other off. Save him and Slocum and the others a lot of work.

"Calm down, Mr. Mitcham," Thane said.

"Stop tellin' me to calm down, dammit!" Mitcham sputtered, and Detroit realized he was at his breaking point.

Swiftly, Thane nodded toward the doorway, where the Chinese servant, Mr. Chan, had been waiting patiently. Mr. Chan took a step toward Mitcham.

Mitcham, catching a glimpse of the movement, wheeled and pulled his gun.

But not fast enough.

Almost quicker than the eye could see, Chan leapt up into the air, launching himself toward Mitcham while spinning and kicking out, all at the same time. His foot connected with Mitcham's hand, and the six-shooter flew into the air, across the room, and collided with a painting of a sailing ship at sea.

The painting fell off the wall with a loud crash at almost the same time that Blackfoot, who had jumped to the side and out of the way, was landing.

It was the dangedest thing Detroit had seen in a long, long time, even neater than that little leg-sweep thing Chan had done to Mitcham during lunch.

Detroit drawled, "Mr. Chan, if'n you wouldn't mind, sometime could you show me how to do that?"

Chan didn't answer. He didn't even look over. His eyes were on Mitcham, who was crawling up off the floor and holding his wrist.

Which was just as well, Detroit mused. He couldn't have pulled off that kick in a million years.

"Goddamn Chink!" Mitcham growled. "If you busted my wrist, I'll—"

"You'll do what, Mr. Mitcham?" Thane intoned. "And I assure you, your wrist is not broken. Is it, Mr. Chan?"

"Not broken," said the little servant, still eyeing Mitcham.

Just like a Mojave rattler waitin' to strike, thought Detroit.

"I am very disappointed in you, gentlemen," Thane continued. He moved his bulk toward the bar, then stopped and turned to Detroit. "Mr. Detroit, you know where things are. Would you care to pour us two brandies?"

Detroit was a little surprised, but he didn't let it show. Tossing his hat to the seat of his chair, he walked over to the bar and pulled down two snifters.

Behind him, he caught just a peek as Mitcham went to retrieve his gun. That Mr. Chan had sure taken the wind out of his sails, all right. But Detroit suspected—

no, knew—that Mitcham wasn't a man to suffer humiliation lightly, especially two humiliations in one day. And then there was the added aggravation of being dressed down by his employer . . .

Things weren't looking too good, Detroit thought as he held out the first brandy snifter to Thane. They weren't looking too terrible bad, but not too good, either.

He sure wished he knew what Slocum was up to.

23

While O'Brien was carving the last of the lamb into slices for sandwiches, Latham Siler was sawing at the last of his bonds. He felt the final strands give all of a sudden, and when they did, a new jolt of pain went through his shoulder, just from the change in position.

He sat there a moment, counting to ten through clenched teeth while he slowly adjusted the shoulder's position and brought it to hang down at his side. Once the worst of the throbbing stopped, he leaned forward—quite careful to keep his arm still—and began to work at the ropes tying his feet together.

Now he had some purchase and the angle wasn't so bad, and he managed to cut his way through these in less then five minutes.

He sure wished he'd listened to his old man's admonitions to always keep his pocketknife honed, though. If he lived through this damned thing, he would. He promised.

Finally, the rope gave up and gave way. He folded the knife and slipped it back into his pocket. Then, grasping his injured arm to his side, he gained his feet.

The shed he was locked into was for tools, and it was fairly small. He rattled the door, but only succeeded in knocking a shovel over, which landed on his boot.

"Dammit!" he hissed, jumping backward—and into something pointy. He moved forward again, this time more carefully.

He put his eye to a crack in the wall and surveyed the territory. It looked like they'd taken every last sheep inside the barn with them, because the only animals in the corral were a couple of milk cows, a nanny goat and Siler's horse.

Well, thank the Lord for small miracles. They hadn't even bothered to strip its tack off, and it was still saddled and bridled. The horse stood with its head down, and snow was building up in the saddle seat. Siler's rifle was still in its boot, his coat still tied behind the saddle.

Now all he had to do was figure out how to get free of this shed. He'd heard one of them say that the wood was rotted, so he figured it'd be easy enough to kick down, but how quietly? He couldn't take a chance on them hearing him.

Finally, and with a near stroke of genius—at least, for him—Siler took out his pocketknife again and slid the blade in the crack between the frame and the door. He worked it up until it touched the bar stick through the latch. If he was lucky—and he seemed to be, so far—it was just a little crosspiece, and would be easily knocked out of its moorings by a simple upward motion.

He held his breath and tried it.

The board moved.

Smiling, he lifted the crossbar up and up, and then heard it hit the ground outside. The door slowly creaked open, letting in a blast of frigid air—but also letting Siler out.

All that was left of the Harper house was a pile of blackened timbers and a few hot spots. They hissed and spat, but still glowed, under the assault of softly falling snowflakes the size of goose down.

Stealthily, still holding his bad arm, Siler headed toward the corral.

Once again, Thane had sent Mitcham and Blackfoot out and kept Detroit behind.

Thane and Blackfoot were to head toward the O'Brien place, which had been their second attack site all along, until they lost Siler and headed back for new orders.

Detroit was a frustrated man. Sure, he was inside and warm and he had a brandy in his hand, but he couldn't get to Slocum, couldn't get to anybody. The worst thing about a situation was not knowing what the hell was going on. At least, the part you cared about.

And right how, that was Slocum and the others. Not Thane's brandy.

"Have you finished your drink, Mr. Detroit?" Thane asked abruptly. Neither of them had spoken for the last ten minutes or so.

Detroit took a last gulp. Shame to do that with

brandy, but maybe Thane was going to send him someplace. He hoped. He needed a chance to ride to the O'Brien place and get that stopped, if Slocum wasn't already there.

"Yes, I am," he said, and rising, he took his glass back over to the bar and put it down. "That be all for now? Like to go check my horse."

"Mr. Detroit, would you consider Mr. Mitcham a good judge of character?" came Thane's unexpected question.

"For real?" Detroit asked.

"Speak freely."

"Well, no, sir, I sure wouldn't," Detroit said. "He's too stuck on himself to see much of anybody else clear."

Thane nodded. "Would you consider him an intelligent man?"

"Depends on how you're definin' intelligent," Detroit said. "Would he make a scholar? No, sir, he wouldn't. Not by a long shot. But if you're talking about smart the other way, the practical way?" Detroit paused. "Well, he's gotta be about forty, mayhap forty-five, and he's still alive. That says somethin' about his skill for survivin' in a hard trade."

"As I thought. Thank you, Mr. Detroit, for your honesty."

"Yes, sir," Detroit said, and picked up his hat. "You want I should follow 'em over to the O'Brien spread, or you got another job for me?"

"Another job, Mr. Detroit. I want you to stand in the front hall."

This time, O'Brien couldn't hold the perplexed look from his face. "Huh? The front hall?" Had Thane lost his marbles?

That was, if he'd ever had them in the first place, which Detroit was doubting more and more as time went along.

Thane nodded curtly. "I wish you to stay here and guard the house. You may stay inside, out of the cold." His eyes flicked out the window. "And snow. It seems we are going to have an unusually unpleasant winter."

Detroit said, "Okay. You want I should make a patrol or two around the house?" He figured this was reasonable.

But Thane said, "No. Stay inside. I'm afraid I must insist. I—not to mention Mr. Chan—would feel much more comfortable knowing you are near."

"Yes, sir," Detroit said. He supposed he could always wait till they were asleep, then sneak out. Damn, he wished he knew where Slocum was!

"That all for now?" he asked.

"Yes," Thane said. And then, as an afterthought, he added, "You may take a chair with you, if you wish. And leave the door open, if you please."

Wordlessly, Detroit grabbed a straight-backed chair from against the wall and carried it from the room. He set it up the hall and back from the door a little way, but before he could sit down, he heard Thane say, "Where I can see you, please. It would ease my mind."

"Yes, sir," Detroit said. He no longer had just suspicions about Thane. All the questions about Mitcham, and now this? There was no doubt about it. Thane didn't trust him any farther than he could pick him up and toss him. Or at least, Detroit was going to have to do something to prove himself before he regained Thane's full confidence.

Detroit dragged his chair into the fan of light created by the open parlor door and sat down, facing the front door and the porch.

"Better," said Thane.

Detroit just grunted. He knew he couldn't count on Thane going to bed anytime soon. If at all.

He supposed he could just shoot the son of a bitch and take off, but without knowing what Slocum had planned for Thane, it was more chance than he cared to take. Slocum could be a headstrong, stubborn old bastard, but he usually knew what he was doing, knew the best and smartest way out of just about anything.

Detroit didn't want to take the chance of tripping him up.

So he bit his tongue and kept his gun in its holster. He sat there and waited.

Slocum wolfed down his sandwich before he mounted up again, and he noticed that Josh had done the same. Josh still looked hungry, though. Big surprise. Well, they didn't have time to break for a five-course dinner. There was trouble coming.

"All right," he said, once the four men were mounted and in the yard. "I figure that Thane's gonna have those boys out here again. They may not have even gone back to his ranch after that little trip-up at the Harpers'. So I want everybody alert, and everybody quiet. Everybody keeps his eyes wide, too."

"Got it," said Deputy Clancy, thumbing the trigger strap off his gun.

"Still the same plan?" O'Brien asked. "Guerilla-type?"

"Check," answered Slocum. "We're gonna take 'em like true sons of the South. Jump out of the trees if we have to. Pop up from behind bushes. Josh, boy, you up to this?"

Josh nodded. Not with too much spirit, but he nodded.

Slocum knew just how he felt: more than likely the way Slocum himself had felt when he rode into his first battle of the War. He'd been so scared that he thought he might shit himself, right there at the beginning. But once the thing was underway, and men were coming at him with rifles blazing and their bayonets threatening, he forgot all about being scared and settled down to the business of staying alive.

He figured it would be the same for Josh. And Josh needed to do this thing, whether he knew it or not. He needed to at least see Mitcham die, or for the rest of his life he'd sit back there on that farm in Iowa, half a man, full of regrets.

As they quietly started their mounts out of the yard and up toward the Thane place, Slocum saw a shadowy figure, half-blurred by the falling snow, come to the door of the bunkhouse. It was old Juanito.

He had several dogs on his heels, one of which Slocum recalled as O'Brien's favorite. The dog took a step out onto the porch, but Juanito said something soft and unintelligible to it, and the dog reluctantly turned around and went back inside.

As they passed him, Juanito took off his hat and spoke. This time, Slocum made out the words.

"Go with God, señores. Go with God."

Siler had mounted his horse with some trouble, but once his shoulder settled down—from an intense pounding that threatened to steal his consciousness again, to something more toward a dull roar—he started off in the direction of Thane's.

Every beat of his horse's hooves jarred his shoulder and shot spears of pain up and down his arm, so he kept his pace slow. He also stopped, once he was out of sight of what was left of the Harper place, to jury-rig a sort of sling for his arm.

It helped immobilize it some, although he had to tie up that jacket funny, and leave part of his side exposed to the elements. But it helped enough that he could travel at a slow jog instead of a walk.

The snow was really coming down now, falling in

a straight line to the ground in big, soft flakes. It would be worse than last night, Siler thought. Might even turn into a full-fledged storm.

His visibility wasn't any too good. He wasn't sure if it was because of the snow, or because he'd lost so much blood. He finally decided it was some of each.

Siler clung to the saddle horn, holding it and his reins in the same hand whenever possible, and guided his horse with tiny shifts of his weight and his legs. He sure hoped that somebody at Thane's place was good at fixing wounds, because he had a feeling that his shoulder was awful torn up.

More than anything, he wanted a soft bed and a bottle of whiskey, both to warm him and to help him forget his pain. Maybe enough to make him pass out for the next week and a half.

Now, he wasn't certain who he was madder at, Detroit for crossing them, or Mitcham and Blackfoot for deserting him. He sort of got to thinking that he should be the most mad at Mitcham and Blackfoot. After all, Detroit was sort of a friend of his, even if he had cleaned him out at poker. And at least Detroit spoke to him like he was a person and not a piece of goddamn furniture.

But hell. The way he was feeling now, he'd just as soon plug the first man he came across, whether it be Detroit, Mitcham or Blackfoot.

A killing right now would make him feel a good bit better. And after all, it was his left shoulder that was stove up. He could still shoot. Well, not so good with a rifle, but he'd taken his spare pistol from his saddlebags, checked the chamber and stuck it in his holster before he'd even gotten on his horse.

He rode on, through the thickening snow.

24

"I'm tellin' you," Mitcham insisted, "there's somethin' screwy about that Chink."

Blackfoot pulled his collar higher up on his neck. "You think there's something wrong with everything," he said flatly.

The snow, which had started out as just a thin white dust, was steadily harder to see through, colder and more dense. The air had taken on a damp quality, too. Not damp, like regular a New Mexico flurry, but thick and almost humid, if cold air could feel that way.

At least, that's what it felt like to Mitcham: as if he could cut the air with his knife and steam would rise from it, like a wound on a fresh kill.

"I don't like this snow," he said, tugging at his glove. They were traveling at a walk. No sense in taking a chance on a horse stepping in an unseen hole out here. Especially now, when the snow had blanketed the ground in white.

Blackfoot didn't say anything.

"I tell you," said Mitcham, "it's gonna turn into somethin' worse than last night. A blizzard, maybe. Goddamn job. I'd like to wring Thane's neck. Right after I wring Detroit's."

Still, the half-breed said nothing. He reined his

horse around a suspicious hump of snow, and didn't bother to acknowledge Mitcham with so much as a grunt.

At last, he said, "Maybe you like to wring my neck, too."

Mitcham scowled. "Don't be a jackass." He looked skyward, and was rewarded by a large clump of flakes landing right square in his eyeball. He blinked rapidly and shook his head, then said, "Dammit, I don't like this snow. Don't like it one bit."

"You never like anything," Blackfoot said. "Me, I like it. Good cover. We can make a clean thing of this tonight. Slip in, kill O'Brien, slip out. With the Harpers burnt out and O'Brien dead and the rest of the sheep men scared the same things will happen to them, tonight will finish the thing, guaranteed. I am glad. I want to go home to Texas. I don't like the snow, but tonight, the snow is good."

"Sweet Jesus Christ!" said Mitcham. "I believe that's about the longest speech I've heard you make in the whole of our acquaintanceship, Blackfoot."

Blackfoot grunted.

Slocum, O'Brien, Josh, and Clancy trudged on through the deepening snow. It had gone from just a tinge of white on the ground to swiftly growing drifts, and the flakes of it, which had fallen straight and true from the sky, were now coming down in thick, twisting flurries, at an angle, blown by a gathering wind. They were coming in clumps, too.

"This ain't good," said Deputy Clancy, his coat pulled snug and his chin tucked down into the wool lining. White flakes dribbled from the brim of his hat like water in a storm.

"We can't split up," he went on. "Least we can't if we ever wanna find each other again. I don't know about you fellers, but I'm sorta opposed to freezin' to death out here all by my lonesome."

"You'd feel better if we froze with you, then?" O'Brien asked. He had his spare hand tucked under his armpit, despite his heavy gloves.

"That's about the size of it," Deputy Clancy said flatly, his words, as before, accompanied by a great deal of vapor.

"All right, boys," Slocum said. He didn't much care for this storm either—for that was what it was turning into—and in his boots, his feet felt frozen solid, but he didn't let on.

"We can't split up," he continued. "Deputy Clancy's got a point. So the plan's changed. Forget the guerrilla warfare. I don't know about you, but when I'm up a tree or hidin' in a ditch, I like to see who—and what—I'm jumpin' on. I ain't gonna waste a rebel yell on a pronghorn."

"So what do we do?" asked Josh, his teeth chattering.

"We're not gonna pick them off in the field," Slocum replied. "We're still riding for the Thane place, but we'll wait until the storm chases 'em back. We'll wait outside. And then . . . then we'll play it by ear."

Deputy Clancy looked annoyed. "That the best you can do, Slocum?"

"Right now, it is."

Uneasily, but never letting it show, Detroit watched Chan quietly come down the stairs, pass him without a word, then go into the parlor and close the door behind him.

Detroit's first impulse was to bolt out the front door, get his horse and ride after Blackfoot and Mitcham. But something held him back. It was something about the murmur of voices issuing from behind the door.

Silently, he rose, went over and put his ear to the keyhole.

"You're sure he can't hear?" Thane was saying.

"Yes, I'm certain, you idiot," Chan said, although it took Detroit a half second to realize it was him. Gone was the singsong Chinese patois, gone from his voice was the tone of a cowering servant. "Now, what are you going to do about that one out in the hall?"

"You heard what Mitcham said at dinner," Thane said. "His horse came in hot last night. Seems to me like a lot more riding than he'd do just scouting cattle and sheep."

"And perhaps he simply did a better job of it than Mitcham and Blackfoot," Chan said flatly.

"Oh," Thane said. Mitcham could practically hear him squirming his toe into the rug. "Well, I just wanted to be on the safe side."

"And you thought the safe side was to leave him here, armed, with us."

"Sorry," said Thane. "Didn't think about it."

There came an angry sputter in Chinese, absolutely none of which Detroit could even try to make out, and then, in English, Chan said, "That's your trouble, Vance. You would think that after all these years, you would have learned how to plan ahead for a period longer than five minutes."

"Sorry," Thane repeated.

Without realizing it, Mitcham, his ear plastered to the keyhole, was smiling. Why, Thane was nothing but a beard! It was Chan's operation, right from the git-go. "Detroit has a smart mouth, but he was vouched for by the late Mr. Siler, whose death might have been avoided had you sent Mr. Detroit along. And as for Mr. Mitcham, I think we would be better off putting an end to him as soon as he has fulfilled his usefulness. I do not trust a man with such a quick temper."

"Yes, sir. Sorry, sir."

Detroit quietly sat back in his chair and resumed his former position, and a few seconds later, Chan opened the parlor door. He bowed, and said, singsong fashion, "Missah Thane, he want to see you, Missah Detroit."

Detroit rose. "Thanks, Mr. Chan," he said. It always paid to be polite to the boss, he thought, silently chuckling, and entered the parlor.

If Thane had been bothered or embarrassed by that

little dressing down he'd just received, he gave no sign. He simply said, "Have a seat, Mr. Mitcham."

Siler's horse kept plowing through the drifts, both large and small. Its mane was crusty with ice, and a person could have barely told that it was a bay. Siler thought that he must look like a half-dead snowman, mounted on a snow horse.

With the emphasis on half-dead.

Still, he forged ahead.

He had seen no one on the way back. No one following him, and no one in the distance. He'd expected to see Blackfoot or Mitcham, anyway. Of course, right now, he was lucky to see ten feet ahead.

But he'd always had a good homing instinct, kinda of like one of those pigeons. Just point him in the right direction, and he'd find his way to whatever he was looking for.

It was a gift, his daddy always used to say.

Well, it had best work tonight, or he'd be frozen like a fish in a shallow pond.

He'd lost all feeling in his side, where it wasn't covered by the jacket, and his shoulder had eased off a good bit, too. Likely from the cold, he figured. He was looking forward to getting into the warmth of Thane's house and letting it hurt like a son of a bitch again. At least there would be whiskey.

And if Thane didn't offer it this time, he'd shoot the son of a bitch and get it himself.

He wondered again if that Chink of Thane's was any good at doctoring. He sure hoped so.

He had just spotted the house lights twinkling in the distance, off through the snow, when he all-of-a-damn-sudden fell off his horse. Wasn't thrown, wasn't bucked, just plain fell. And he fell on his bad shoulder to boot.

At least his horse didn't run off.

He sat there a minute in the drift, his eyes tearing and the tears freezing as fast as they were formed.

"Damn!" he said aloud as the pain shot through him over and over. "Goddamn son of a mother of a bitch dog cur!"

His horse spooked at the sound, but Siler caught the reins before he could bolt away.

"Sorry, goddammit," he muttered. "I'm just tryin' to get us both someplace warm, all right?"

He was surely earning his pay this time, he thought angrily as he pulled himself up into a stand by hanging on to the stirrup. Then he stood there, in the shelter of the horse's body, gathering his strength for the next expenditure.

"Horse," he whispered, just over the wind, if we get through this, I'm gonna take care of all of them. Detroit, Mitcham, and that Blackfoot. Maybe Thane and his Chink, too."

With a tremendous effort and a shout of "God *damn* it!" he heaved himself up and over the saddle. He waited a moment, muttering "Whoa, horse. Ho, boy, easy." And then he turned, swinging his right leg over to the other side at the same time.

His foot found the other stirrup. He gathered his

reins. He felt the blackness crawling over his brain once more, and put his head down on his saddle horn until it passed.

Detroit was just standing up again after his little talk with Thane.

He had to admit that Thane was one hell of a bullshitter. He'd made it sound real convincing and logical, when the truth of it was that he'd fouled up and was backtracking, trying to make it right with his boss.

Detroit would have bet that Thane was a helluva poker player. Or could have been, if he'd ever tried. Then he decided no, if Thane ever sat down on one of those spindly barroom chairs, he'd likely crush it into splinters.

His hat still in his hands, Detroit nodded in a semblance of a bow. "I'll get right on it, Mr. Thane." He couldn't help but throw in "You sure you folks'll be all right unguarded?"

"No, no," Thane said. "We shall be all right. I think it's more important for you to be out there, going after O'Brien."

"If you think so, sir," Detroit said, his grin just itching to get out. Wait until he told Slocum!

He was leaving the parlor and stepping into the foyer when there was a commotion out on the porch, and he swung open the front door to find Siler on the porch floor, leaned up against the doorjamb. He'd fallen there, by the look and sound of it.

"Could I get some help out here?" Detroit called, and Mr. Chan materialized beside him.

"You take arms, I take legs," the Chinaman said.

Detroit simply obeyed.

They dragged Siler into the parlor, got his coat over him and a whiskey down his throat, although most of it ended up on his shirt. Mr. Chan went to the kitchen to heat some water.

"He's shot up bad," Detroit said, gently probing the injury. "He's got a busted shoulder, from what I can tell. Slug did a lot of damage. And it looks like he's got some frostbite, to boot."

Siler, who was not yet all the way conscious, tried to move his lips.

"Can't hear you, buddy," Detroit said. "Say it again." He put his ear close to Siler's mouth.

This time, he heard what Siler was trying to say. It was "You . . . goddamn . . . traitor."

"What?" asked Thane, from across the room, where he had remained ever since Detroit and Chan had brought Siler in. If Thane backed up any farther, Detroit thought, he'd break down the wall and be in the next room. "What is it? Does he want something?"

"Water," Detroit said with a perfectly straight face. "He wants water. But I think we'd best knock him out with whiskey. He's better off unconscious until you can get a doc out here to look at that shoulder. Must hurt like all get-out. You wanna pour him out another? Make it a tumblerful this time."

25

"I can't see a damned thing."

"M-me neither," Mitcham replied through chattering teeth. "Can't you smell your way there or s-somethin'? You're the Indian."

"Half," said Blackfoot, an edge of irritation coming through in his voice. "I didn't get the part that smells directions."

They both sat there, facing into the bitter wind, blinking away the furiously blowing flakes and looking through squinted eyes into nothing but a sea of white: white ground, white air, white forever.

"What now?" Mitcham asked. He was pissed that they hadn't had done with it yet, pissed at the weather, pissed at Blackfoot for not getting them there. He was also pissed at Thane and that Chink and Detroit. Actually, at most everybody. But they could wait. Right at the moment, he just wanted to take care of O'Brien and get paid.

After he finished up here, he wouldn't be back in this vicinity for a long time. No, make that forever.

Goddammit, anyhow!

To his right, Blackfoot started to move his horse forward. Mitcham was careful to keep shoulder to shoulder with him. With snow this bad, you were liable to lose a man if he got so far away that you couldn't reach out and touch him.

"Where you goin?" Mitcham shouted over the wind.

Blackfoot pointed ahead. "Trees, I think."

Great. Now he was seeing trees.

But when a split-second lull came in the storm, when the wind was thinking about changing direction then didn't, Mitcham saw them, too. Just a glimpse of some vertical shapes looming near. It was enough to convince him, though.

"We gonna wait it out?" he hollered.

The Indian nodded, right before his horse walked straight into a tree.

Whether he realized it or not, Slocum and his companions had a distinct advantage. The wind was at their backs.

Of course, Josh didn't see it. He clung like a tick to his saddle, and Slocum wasn't sure if the kid was paralyzed with cold or fear. Maybe both.

Deputy Clancy, who you'd think was more accustomed to this kind of weather, had his head snugged down so far into his collar that it looked like he had no neck.

And O'Brien? Well, he, at least, had come prepared. There was a wool muffler wrapped round his neck and pulled up over the lower half of his face. His hat was pulled low, and somewhere along the way, he'd tied it down—and covered up his ears—

with a second muffler. His coat was heavier than any of the others', and he'd pulled on a second pair of pants over the first when they'd stopped at his place for sandwiches.

At the time, Slocum had thought he was just plain being a nervous Nellie. That much corduroy and denim on his legs would just slow him down if they had to run for cover or something. That muffler around his neck would make it difficult for him to turn his head quickly.

Now Slocum realized that O'Brien had known what he was doing. At least, if they never found Thane's men or Thane's place, if the rest of them froze to death out here, stiff as three hides stretched out to dry, O'Brien would be alive to tote their carcasses back to civilization.

He'd look funny in all that padding, but he'd be alive.

As it was, O'Brien had taken the lead, and they plodded along behind, following the trail his horse blazed through the drifts, trusting that he could find the way.

And he did, much to Slocum's surprise. He reined in at the top of a hill and waited for the others to catch up. Slocum was the first to so do, and gazed down into the valley below, at the infrequently glimmering—but nonetheless there—lights.

"Well, I'll be damned!" he shouted to O'Brien. "Good job."

O'Brien shrugged, or at least he seemed to, under all

that padding. He pulled down his mouth muffler long enough to say, "I could have ridden here in my sleep."

"All right," Slocum said, forgetting the cold now that the quarry was in sight. "We ride down real quiet. First, we go to the barn and check for Blackfoot and Mitcham's horses."

"How do you know what they ride?" O'Brien shouted, this time through his muffler.

"Saw 'em," Slocum replied. At least, he'd caught a peek at part of them. Enough, anyway, to know that Mitcham rode a blood red bay, and Blackfoot rode a black with tall hind stockings.

"Let's go, then," shouted O'Brien.

Slocum threw a look Josh's way. The kid seemed all right. He seemed dead set on it, in fact.

Sticking close, they all began to pick their way down the slope, toward the barn.

Detroit's plan to get Siler unconscious by feeding him whiskey wasn't working very well. He had no way of knowing that Siler had been hitting the bottle secretly, each and every night, or that he was a bottomless pit for alcohol.

So no matter how much booze he forced down Siler's throat, he never got much drunker.

And the son of a bitch kept trying to talk! Luckily, Thane reacted to the wounded man the way a woman reacts to a rat in the house, and hadn't come any closer. But Chan, the mastermind, was a different matter.

He hauled in the water, dropped a fistful of clean rags next to Siler and said, "I clean."

Slocum found no evidence of Mitcham or Blackfoot's horses in the barn, but insisted that the men bring their own mounts out back behind the house, where they wouldn't be spied if the two fled the storm and came on back.

When at last they all met up again—having taken an assortment of circuitous routes around the ranch house—they huddled near the back door.

"Josh," Slocum said, "you and O'Brien wait three minutes, then go on it. Head for the parlor. That's where it looks like everybody is. Everybody that's home so far, I mean. Me and Deputy Clancy'll take the front. That all right with you, Clancy?"

Clancy shrugged. "Don't make me no nevermind, just as long as we get inside and out of this blow. Anybody else notice that the snow's stoppin'?"

"Getting too cold to snow," O'Brien said.

Nobody, not even O'Brien, seemed to take any comfort in that.

"All right," Slocum said. "Let's move. Three minutes, remember."

Josh nodded.

O'Brien did the same, but he had his watch out and was staring at it.

Slocum and Clancy moved quietly away, along the side of the house.

• • •

"I've had it with this shit," Mitcham said through a haze of foggy breath. "I'm goin' back."

He reined his horse from the little glade in which he and Blackfoot had taken shelter, and began to follow his rapidly disappearing tracks back toward Thane's place.

The hell with this job. He was going to go back, take care of that goddamn Chink, rob Thane, take off and change his name again. Shooting sheep was low enough, but doing it in the middle of a goddamn blizzard?

Enough was enough.

He heard Blackfoot's nag plowing along, too, right behind him. Good. Blackfoot was about as loyal as a tarantula, and would likely go along with everything he wanted to do. It would be good to have another set of hands to help. Especially with that goddamn servant.

"Going to stop snowing," he heard Blackfoot say.

The snow had, indeed, thinned some, but it didn't show any sign of stopping. At least, to Mitcham.

"Why?" he asked.

"Getting too cold," came the terse response.

"We'll see," said Mitcham.

They trudged on.

Slocum and Clancy came in low, kneeling beneath the windows, until they had reached the front door.

"How we doin' on time?" Slocum whispered.

Clancy checked his watch, then shoved it back in his

pocket. "Just about right. 'Bout ten seconds to go."

"Close enough," said Slocum, and tried the front door's latch. It was open. He pulled his gun, and Clancy did the same.

"Ready?" asked Slocum.

The deputy nodded. "Let's go."

Siler was still mumbling as Chan bulled his way in with a damp rag. Detroit could only hope that the language barrier, plus Siler's slurred words, would keep his secret from getting out. Why the hell couldn't Siler have fallen off his horse someplace out there?

He backed up and stood close behind the China-man, where he could hopefully hear every mumble that came from Siler's mouth.

His hand was resting on the butt of his gun, just in case.

"No understand, no understand," Chan was saying.

Siler tried harder.

"No hear, no understand."

Siler motioned Chan closer.

This is it, dammit, thought Detroit, and he started to quietly step back, lifting his gun from the holster as he did.

A blast of cold air came from the parlor doors, and they all—excepting Siler—looked up.

"Mr. Mitcham?" called Thane. "Mr. Blackfoot?"

Slocum appeared in the doorway, both his pistols leveled. Deputy Clancy was right next to him.

The cavalry arrives, thought Detroit with a grin.

"It's over, Thane," Slocum intoned. "Hands on your head. Tell your man to do the same."

Detroit was just about to open his mouth to warn Slocum about Mr. Chan, when the little Chinaman gave an earsplitting whoop and launched himself toward the doorway.

Clancy was so startled that he hopped back a good three feet at just about the moment that Chan launched himself into the air and kicked Slocum, hard, right in the center of his chest.

Slocum went to his knees, all the air knocked from him, and Chan took advantage of the situation by kicking Slocum again, this time in the side of his head.

Almost quicker than Detroit could register, the Chinaman had slapped the gun from Clancy's hand, brought him down with a side-sweep of his leg and chopped him across the back of his neck with the side of his hand.

Belatedly, Detroit drew his gun.

Thane was moving toward his desk as fast as he could, which wasn't too awful fast, and Detroit shot at the Chinaman first, then wheeled to shoot Thane. His slug took Thane in the lower arm, and he clasped it, then collapsed to his knees with a floor-shaking thud.

Detroit wheeled back toward Chan again, only to see the sole of Chan's foot as it rushed up to connect with the point of his chin. He heard something crunch, and then everything went black.

26

Slocum shook his head. That didn't clear it, and he shook it again. He heard the sound of a scuffle coming from across the room, and picked up his gun, aiming it in the general direction of the sound. The Chinaman had knocked him silly and his vision wasn't up to par, but his mind was.

And as he tried to focus on the black-pajamaed Chinaman, he shouted, "O'Brien, where are you, dammit!"

The black blur turned toward him and began another rush. Slocum aimed at the center of it and fired, then fired again before the man's body struck him.

But this time, there were no thrashing feet, no deadly hands. He simply fell, limp, into Slocum's arms.

Slocum was just pushing him off as O'Brien and Josh burst up the back hall.

"Sorry," O'Brien said breathlessly.

"The dang back door was locked," added Josh. Then he said, "Who's that?"

"Damned if I know," Slocum said. His vision was clearing a little more now. "Josh, get in there and check on Detroit and Thane. O'Brien, see if the deputy's still alive."

While they went about their business, Slocum pulled himself back until he was leaning up against the side of the staircase. He gave his head another shake, and at last, everything came back into focus.

More or less, anyhow.

He reached over and felt the Chinaman's neck for a pulse, just in case, but he was dead. What the hell was that stuff he was doing, anyhow? He'd seen Chinese pull some pretty amazing stunts over in San Francisco, but nothing like this. Those were mostly crippling chops to the arms on the neck, but without the kicking. Well, he supposed he'd never know now.

"He's alive," O'Brien said, looking up from Clancy.

As if to underscore it, Clancy groaned, then felt his head. "Jesus H. What happened?"

"Damned if I know," Slocum answered truthfully. Reaching up to grab a stair spindle, he hoisted himself to his feet. "Josh?"

"I think Detroit's jaw is busted," he replied, "and he's out like a light. Thane's only hit in the arm, but he's good an' passed out, too."

"First thing," Slocum said, "let's pull those curtains. Don't want Blackfoot and Mitcham ridin' up and seein' us big as life through the windows."

Josh got busy pulling curtains.

"Next," said Slocum, "let's get these boys put away. It'll take two of us to haul Thane."

O'Brien nodded and followed Slocum into the parlor. Together, they managed to drag Thane's enormous bulk down the hall, to the dining room, where Slocum bound him to the china closet, then gagged him, just in case he came to.

When they came back up the hall, Clancy was on his feet and still rubbing his face. He worked his jaw around and around, pausing long enough to say, "Damn!"

"I know just how you feel," Slocum said. His chest ached like a son of a bitch. "This one, too," he added, pointing to the servant.

"That one, I can handle myself," O'Brien said. He bent over and hoisted the body, tossing it over his shoulder like an errant ewe, and trudged off down the hall again.

"What now?" asked Josh. All the curtains were drawn. Detroit still lay on the floor, unconscious, and Siler lay muttering on the sofa.

Slocum could make out just enough of it to figure Siler had overheard something, either while they were putting out the fire, or later on. Slocum turned to Josh and said, "Gag him."

"Right," said a voice: Detroit's, from the floor where he was still lying. He touched his jaw with the tip of his finger, and it looked like every gentle poke hurt like hell. Slocum cringed for him.

"Right what?" Slocum asked. "And answer me easy. I think that jaw of yours is busted."

"No shit," Detroit mumbled. Now he was holding his jaw with both hands. "This is sure as hell a retirement party I'm always gonna remember," he said to himself, and then raised his volume a little, adding, "Son of a bitch found out about me somehow. I was tryin' to get him drunk, but he's a bottomless pit for whiskey. You fellers showed up just in time. And now, if'n nobody minds, I'm gonna shut the hell up."

Deputy Clancy said, "Can you get up? Just nod yes or no."

Detroit nodded in the affirmative.

"Then c'mon. I'll get that bound up for you good and tight. It'll hold you, at least till you can see the doc."

The two of them left the room, the deputy supporting Detroit, who was still a little woozy, and Slocum was left alone with Josh.

Slocum sighed. He didn't know how long it'd be until Mitcham and Blackfoot showed up, but they were going to show sooner or later. Now, Mitcham was wanted dead or alive, but Slocum didn't know about Blackfoot. There should have been a bounty on him, and a big one at that, but that didn't mean there was one. Deputy Clancy hadn't said one way or the other.

He turned to Josh. "For now," he said, "you go upstairs and find a window that looks out over the front of the house. Watch for 'em."

Josh nodded. Having lived through that last scuffle had made him a little braver, Slocum thought, because the nod was curt and confident. Josh went up the stairs, and Slocum went to find O'Brien and the deputy.

He found them in the dining room, where Clancy was binding Detroit's jaw shut. O'Brien looked on. He'd lit his pipe.

"Deputy?" Slocum said.

Clancy looked up. "Last time I heard. Although now I'm sorta thinkin' that this little adventure might impress the citizenry enough that I'll be sheriff come next election."

"Could well be, boy," said O'Brien, nodding.

"Is there any reward on Blackfoot?" Slocum asked. "I already know about Mitcham."

The deputy didn't miss a beat. "Two thousand New Mexico, four thousand Arizona, and three in the Colorado Territory. Might be others, but that was all I found so far. You boys been keeping me away from my posters."

"How's he wanted?"

"Same as Mitcham. Dead or alive."

Slocum slowly blew a long sigh out through his nostrils. This was to the death, then. Nobody'd have to take any chances to keep Mitcham or Blackfoot alive. He said, "All right. I've got Josh upstairs, watchin' the front. Been thinkin', too."

"How so?" asked O'Brien around his pipe stem.

"I think it's gonna look too funny with all the blinds drawn. I think we need to haul Thane there back in his front room and face him away from the window. They'll see enough of him hangin' over his chair to recognize him. And Bill, you'd best go out and lead Siler's horse around back, with ours."

Thane, who had regained consciousness some-where during the proceedings, tried to speak, his eyes wide—terrified, Slocum thought—but the gag in his mouth put a quick end to that.

"What's he tryin' to say?" asked Clancy.

Slocum grabbed him under one arm, and O'Brien took the other. "I don't give a shit," Slocum replied. "Now, heave!"

Mitcham and Blackfoot rode down into the ranch yard fairly easily. At least they could see where they were going, almost as clear as day. It had stopped snowing altogether. It was as still as pond water on a windless day, and the previously blown and drifted snow on the ground, which showed not a mark, reflected the light of the moon and the clear, sparkling stars. But Mitcham was frozen half to death, and didn't mind mentioning it every few minutes.

When they reached the barn, Blackfoot leapt from his horse and tersely said, "I'll put them up. You explain to the fat man."

"If I wasn't so damned cold, I'd never agree to this, y'know," grumbled Mitcham. But still he was looking forward to getting into the warmth of the parlor, even if it meant putting up with a little—or a lot of—wrath from Thane. Besides, he wouldn't have to listen to much of it. Thane would be dead in a few minutes.

He went up toward the house, fighting the drifts which were knee-high in some places. He batted at his arms as he went, trying to get the circulation restarted, and stopped every once in a while to stamp his feet. Never again would he come to New Mexico—or at least, this part of it—in winter, no matter how much money was offered.

He mounted the porch, went down it to the front door and knocked. He was sure he'd seen Thane through the window, sitting there with his fat old back turned toward him. Maybe he'd gone to sleep. Or more likely, he was too goddamn grand to get up off his ass.

Well, it didn't look like the Chink was coming either. He put his hand on the latch and pushed it down. The door swung in. He stood there a minute, looking at it. The back of his neck itched.

Still, he removed his hat and went into the parlor. "Mr. Thane?" he asked.

There was no time for Slocum, hidden behind the coat tree in the dimly lit hall, to call out, "Hold your fire!"

Josh, who had alerted them that Mitcham was on his way up to the house and Blackfoot was on his way to the barn, was halfway down the stairs. In a crouch, he fired through the spindles and caught Mitcham in the arm.

Mitcham, only winged, dropped and rolled as he drew his gun, and returned the fire from behind a heavy parlor chair. Josh toppled down the stairs and lay still.

Cursing beneath his breath, Slocum signaled to Deputy Clancy to go farther down the hall, to the room's far doorway. Slocum stayed where he was.

He couldn't check on Josh, not without entering Mitcham's range of fire. He thought he saw the kid breathing, though.

But Blackfoot was still out there somewhere, and he'd undoubtedly heard the gunplay. Terrific. Why couldn't they have just tied their horses to the rail like the bums they were, instead of stabling them?

He signaled again with an arm, warning Clancy to hold his position and keep quiet. He didn't know where Detroit was. Probably still back in the dining room, holding his jaw. Slocum didn't cast a glance down the hall, though. His eyes were riveted on the front door's latch.

Which was slowly moving.

Slocum flattened against the wall again, his gun drawn, the gleam of its dull steel secreted behind the arm of a coat.

The door opened an inch.

"Mitcham?" came Blackfoot's voice. Slocum had never forgotten it, not after all these years. He particularly remembered the bastard's scream when he fell over that cliff. "Mitcham? You all right?"

"Yeah," came Mitcham's reply. "You see anybody out in that hall?"

The door creaked open a few more inches, and Slocum pulled his head back. He was thinking what a good thing it was that Vance Thane was such a big, fat man who wore such big, fat, heavy coats.

In a moment, he heard Blackfoot holler, "Nobody but a dead kid on the steps."

Slocum's spirits sank. But then, it was fairly dark. Maybe Blackfoot just hadn't seen the kid breathe. Then again, maybe he wasn't breathing anymore.

Some scuffling sounds came from the parlor, as if Mitcham was hoisting himself to his feet. "All right," he said. "Thane?" he asked, as if he'd just noticed that the big man wasn't moving, hadn't turned around.

It was now or never. If both of them got in there, or Mitcham got Thane's gag off, Slocum and his men were in a peck of trouble. He wasn't foolish enough to underestimate Mitcham or Blackfoot's ruthlessness, or their talent for killing.

He popped out from behind the coat rack and fired at Blackfoot, catching him in the chest.

Blackfoot went down to his knees and Slocum fired again, this time directly into the heart. He thought he saw a wave of recognition cross Blackfoot's ugly face, but he couldn't be sure. He hoped Blackfoot had recognized him, though, because just then he fell forward, as dead as a slab of granite.

The only word that came from the parlor was Mitcham's muffled "Shit!" and the sounds of a chair being shoved.

"Clancy!" shouted Slocum. There was no point in hand signals now.

"He's got himself barricaded," Clancy shouted back.

Slocum looked over toward Josh. He had to wait for it, but the kid breathed again. Thank God.

Suddenly, there was a crash of glass and a splintering of wood. Slocum didn't need anybody to tell him that Mitcham had gone through the window, though in the second it took Slocum to sprint to the front door, Clancy shouted, "He's outside!"

Slocum flung open the front door, but stayed back in the shadows. It'd be just like Mitcham to be waiting out there for him.

He had no more than tentatively stuck his nose around the corner of the door frame when a gun fired.

But it didn't hit the door. Or the door frame. Or Slocum. Or even the porch, so far as Slocum could tell.

He chanced another look, then relaxed.

Grover Detroit was just walking up from the barn, holstering his gun. Jack Mitcham lay spread-eagled in the snow, his arms outstretched, his gun far from his fingers, blood rapidly staining the snow.

Through his jaw bandages, Detroit managed to say, "Ain't you gonna congratulate me, Slocum?"

Slocum walked over to the body and kicked the gun even farther away, then rolled the body over with his boot. Mitcham was dead, all right. One bullet, straight through the neck.

"Nice shot," said Slocum as Detroit joined him.

"Was aimin' for his head," Detroit said through clenched teeth.

"Well, I'll be a son of a bitch," said Deputy Clancy,

from behind them. He'd just walked out from the house. "Figured to find at least one'a you dead. Nice surprise."

"How's the kid?" Slocum asked.

"Didn't stop to pat his hand, but he still looks alive enough to me. Collarbone, I think. Or thereabouts."

"Anybody but me want a drink?" Detroit said through strapped-together jaws.

"Yeah, but how you gonna drink it?" Slocum asked.

"Through a funnel, if'n I have to," Detroit replied.

27

Three days later, Slocum found himself waking up in Lola's bed for the last time. She had reservations on the noon stage, and a packet of Slocum's reward money tucked into her valise.

She'd spent most of the night thanking him in her own inimitable fashion.

While she still slept in the crook of Slocum's arm, he still puzzled over the Chan and Thane thing. Sure, he could see Detroit's point about nobody taking a Chinese man seriously when it came to owning land, and particularly cattle ranching. He could even see why Chan had hired Thane to front for him. But try as hard as he might, he couldn't figure out what Chan had against sheep.

Maybe he never would.

The day after the range war ended, Territorial Marshal Steve Fuller had come roaring into town with three deputies, having received Clancy's wire, and primed for a fight. Slocum had the pleasure of dissuading him of that notion, and Fuller had settled for a beer, instead.

Fuller had dutifully—and officially—identified the bodies, and yesterday the reward money for Blackfoot and Mitcham had been wired in by the New Mexico authorities. Siler turned out to be worth a little, too. And Fuller had wired the Arizona Territory, among others, to advise the authorities there.

Trouble was, Slocum and Josh and Detroit would have to go there to pick up their money.

That was no problem for Slocum—or Detroit either, he suspected—but Josh, who was bound up in bandages at the doc's place, wanted to get back to Iowa in the worst possible way.

Slocum had made Josh a deal. He promised to wire him his reward money as it came in. Or as he collected it, more to the point.

"Might take me upwards of a year," Slocum told him.

"I trust you," Josh said with a grin, and that was it.

Detroit's jaw hadn't turned out to be busted, after all. Chan's foot had cracked it good and loosened a few teeth, but the doc said that Grover'd be eating solid food again in no time.

You had to take pity on the man, though. Just when they'd taken the bandages off his head, his mare bit him right square in the ass, and he had to carry a pillow everywhere, just to sit on.

As for Sheriff Davis? Oh, he tried to take the credit, but Detroit and Slocum started talking to a few people around town—and then Marshal Fuller arrived—and low and behold, Sheriff Davis was now citizen Davis. Clancy had been appointed interim sheriff until the